GAME
ON

GAME ON

MATT CAIN

REVIEW

1

'We're doing a media project,' says the manager as he switches off the TV. 'Jackie's going to have a word after lunch.'

Tom Horrocks touches his collar bone. He was gripped by the video analysis of Saturday's game but off the pitch he doesn't want anything to do with the media. 'What's it about?' he asks.

Sergio Santos frowns. When he was appointed manager of Toddington FC, he moved to the UK from his native Spain and he has learned to speak excellent English. But there are still some things he finds confusing. 'I don't know, something about BLG. Or is it BGT?'

'*Britain's Got Talent*?' asks Kyle Skinner, a striker with long hair which he wears up in an Alice band. 'You know I can do a banging pec dance.'

Sergio rakes his fingers through his black quiff, which is flecked with grey. 'Sorry, I must have got the letters mixed up. It's the one to do with gays.'

Tom clenches his jaw.

'LGBT,' offers Nigerian striker Uche Usman,

Toddington FC's captain and star player. 'Or LGBTQ+ as people say now.'

I've got a bad feeling about this, thinks Tom.

'Do you think they'll ask us to play in drag?' Kyle says. 'I can just see you in pink sequins, Uche.'

'Red's more my colour,' Uche says. 'But you'd look great in pink, Kyle. You could do your hair in pigtails.'

Despite Uche's impish grin, Tom senses a crackle of tension. Kyle played centre forward until Uche was bought by Sergio when he came to the club five years ago. Kyle was moved over to the right wing, mainly to provide the assists for Uche to score.

'I don't know any of the details but the media team will explain,' Sergio says. 'Now let's get out on the pitch!'

Tom turns around and picks up the clothes the kit man has laid out for him. The squad are in the dressing room at the training ground, which is between two areas of housing to the west of the town centre. The room is basic, with white walls made of breeze-block, wooden benches and dull grey steel lockers. But the training ground is where the players spend most of their time, and it's where Tom has always felt most at home.

He tugs off his tracksuit and pulls on his kit, including a shirt with the number five. Once he's done up his boots, he takes a quick look at himself in the mirror. His red hair, freckles and Celtic complexion work well with Toddington's purple, unlike lighter colours that make him look washed out.

But Tom has never been one of the team's heartthrobs, which suits him perfectly as it's helped him dodge attention. Nor does he play in any of the hero positions; as a centre back, he's a big, powerful man who forms the heart of the defensive wall. He's also tall, so he can win the headers when the opponents kick the ball long and high. As his dad is fond of saying, he's built to be a defender.

At twenty-eight, Tom has only ever played for Toddington, or the Toddies as they're known. Unlike most of the other players, he grew up in the town and trained at the youth academy before playing for the under eighteens. Eventually he joined the first team and for a few years he quietly lived his dream.

Then Toddington FC was taken over by a group of rich Malaysians. The new money brought about a change of manager and a flurry of transfers. The Toddies were soon promoted from third-tier football to the Championship, then – after two seasons – the all-important Premier League.

Seen as the plucky underdogs and lifted up by the goodwill of the public, they've climbed the league table and are now ranked fourth. If they can just hang on in there, they'll qualify for the UEFA Champions League – something way beyond Tom's childhood dream.

As he trots out onto the grass, he's determined to do everything he can to make that happen. But, as he stretches his muscles, one worry intrudes. *What's this gay thing?* he thinks.

Tom wonders if he can duck out by saying he needs to pick up his daughter from school. *But no,* he remembers, *Sergio asked us to stay.*

As usual, the second Tom's boot touches the ball, his worries disappear and he focuses on football. Today is about recovering from the game the day before so the team are doing ninety minutes of light training – mainly passing exercises, plus some work on team shape.

Once training is over, he and Uche go to the gym for a short workout. The two men have been close ever since the club asked Tom to keep an eye on their new player. Although they're from very different backgrounds, they soon found they have a similar sense of humour.

'Just imagine Kyle's challenged you to a

pec dance-off,' Tom teases as Uche struggles to complete a set of chest flies. 'Imagine his muscles popping up and down.'

Uche tosses his heavy dumbbells onto the floor. 'Mate, I just did a sick in my throat.'

After the gym, Tom and Uche shower, change back into their tracksuits, and go to the canteen.

As they do every day, the club's chefs have prepared lunch with an eye on nutrition rather than taste; today's meal is brown rice, grilled chicken and steamed spinach. Generally, Tom has no problem with the bland food, but today he's lost his appetite.

Uche raises an eyebrow. 'What's up? Are you nervous about this media thing?'

Tom shoots him a glare.

Uche shrugs. 'I was thinking of volunteering. If you don't mind?'

Tom's mouth falls open. But before he can reply, the club's publicist Jackie Broomhead sweeps in, clapping her hands. A blonde woman in her forties, Jackie has a booming voice and a broad Lancashire accent. She announces that Toddington FC is leading this year's Rainbow Laces campaign, the FA's plan to promote greater acceptance for LGBTQ+ people in football. 'The media launch is on Friday. It's not difficult, just some photos and interviews – and obviously

I'll tell you what to say. Now who's going to volunteer?'

Suddenly, the players tuck into their lunch as if it's the most delicious food they've ever tasted. Being asked to take part in media events and charity activities is nothing new, and many of them don't want to give up their time off.

Sergio Santos stands up. 'Do they have to, Jackie? You know what I think about this kind of thing – it's a distraction from the football.'

'Try telling that to the gay players in the Premier League,' Jackie fires back. 'Wait a minute, you can't – because there aren't any. Or at least none who've come out of the closet!'

Sergio scoffs. 'Come on, can you imagine if one of our lads came out of the closet? This place would be a circus!'

Uche pushes his chair back. 'I'll volunteer. I think the campaign's really important.'

Jackie shoots him a beam. 'Oh great! Thanks, flower. Anyone else?'

'As if our fans care about all this crap,' Kyle grumbles. 'The only reason the FA does it is to shut up the woke brigade in London.'

A few other players murmur in vague agreement. Jackie ignores them and continues to look for volunteers.

Tom just wants to slip away. *Oh, please don't notice me*, he thinks.

Jackie signs up two midfielders, promising that if they do this they'll be in the clear for a while. 'Now I just need one more . . .'

Uche leans in to Tom. 'Mate, are you sure you don't fancy it?'

'Are you serious?' Tom hisses.

'You might find it helpful.'

Tom rubs the crease between his eyebrows. Uche is the only person he's told his secret. Uche is the only person who knows he's gay. *And,* Tom thinks, *he doesn't need reminding how I feel about it.*

'Tom!' bellows Jackie. 'You haven't done media in ages. It's your turn, flower.'

Tom manages to nod.

But his stomach dips in dread.

As a closeted gay man, launching a campaign to promote football as a gay-friendly sport is the *last* thing he wants to do.

2

'You're sending me where?' asks Cosmo Roberts.

'Toddington,' replies his boss. 'It's that small town in Lancashire where the football team is suddenly beating the big boys.'

Cosmo blinks. 'Sorry, you lost me at football.' Worried he's overstepped the mark, he flashes Joshua a smile.

'Come on, this is a great opportunity,' Joshua says.

Cosmo runs a finger over his thin moustache. 'Yeah, but am I really the right person? Man, I *hate* football.'

Joshua waves a hand. 'Never mind that. See this as a form of activism.'

I have to hand it to him, thinks Cosmo. *He knows just how to win me round.*

At the age of twenty-six – and just ten months into his job as a reporter on the LGBTQ+ news website QueerAndNow – Cosmo Roberts is full of ambition. All his life, he's considered himself an activist, fighting to bring about social change. And now – finally – he's in a position to do so.

'Rainbow Laces is a really important campaign,' adds Joshua.

Cosmo tugs on a lock of his dark hair, the tips of which he's dyed purple. 'Is it, though? Everyone knows football's homophobic. I don't see how a handful of straight players wearing rainbow-coloured laces will make a difference. If things are going to change, we need a gay player to come out of the closet.'

Joshua rubs his beard. 'Yeah, well, you know I've been chasing that story for years – every queer journalist has. But I don't think it's going to happen. Not yet, anyway.'

Cosmo looks around Joshua's office, which is stuffed full of awards from LGBTQ+ groups, all of them inscribed with the name Joshua Battle, editor of QueerAndNow. Through the window, he sees trains snaking in and out of London Bridge Station, while behind him he can hear the sound of tapping on keyboards coming from the open-plan area.

'I'm sorry but I just don't get it,' Cosmo says. 'Look at what happened to all the Olympic athletes who came out – everyone celebrates them for their bravery.'

Joshua tucks his hands under his armpits. 'Well, maybe it's harder for a footballer.'

'Bollocks! I've no sympathy. And as far as I'm

concerned, any player who doesn't come out is fair game.'

Joshua's eyebrows shoot up to his hairline. 'What? Are you saying we should "out" them?'

'Sorry, no, I'm not saying that. But I do think they're helping prolong a shitty situation. And I don't think we should help the FA with its empty virtue signalling.'

Joshua puts his feet on the desk, revealing a pair of gleaming white trainers that contrast with Cosmo's battered old pair. 'Cosmo, I respect the fact that you care so much about this, but for once you're going to have to put your principles to one side. QueerAndNow is the media partner for Rainbow Laces. I need you to go to this launch.'

Cosmo examines his nails, which his housemate has painted purple to match his hair. *OK,* he thinks, *I've said my piece. Now I should probably do as I'm told.*

He looks up. 'When is it?'

'This Friday.'

Disappointment thumps into Cosmo. 'But I thought we were going to Paris?'

Joshua crinkles his brow. 'Yeah, I need to talk to you about that.'

Oh God, thinks Cosmo, *here we go . . .*

As well as being Joshua's employee, Cosmo has

been having sex with him for eighteen months. The two men first spoke online, before meeting up in real life. Even though Cosmo's usual type is sturdily built, pale men with fair hair and Joshua has a wiry frame and dark colouring, he felt a powerful attraction. He wondered if this could be because Joshua is eight years older than him and more mature than anyone he'd dated before.

Whatever the reason, he soon found out that they were a great match in the bedroom. And not just that but Joshua sparked his brain and seemed interested in his political views. When they were together, Cosmo felt more confident, more driven.

If only he didn't have a boyfriend, he thought.

To give Joshua his due, he did tell Cosmo he had a boyfriend, after their third hook-up. But he insisted they had an open relationship. At first, Cosmo hadn't wanted to carry on seeing him, but Joshua had convinced Cosmo he was being old-fashioned and stuffy. He insisted that his set-up was more modern and open-minded.

Despite his doubts, Cosmo had given in. But he'd built up feelings for Joshua. He'd tried to bury them, telling himself to stop being so basic, so *needy*. But he couldn't. *And now Joshua has just gone and trampled on my feelings*, he thinks.

Cosmo steadies his breathing before opening his mouth. 'But Josh—'

'Babe,' Joshua interrupts, 'you know I hate being called Josh.'

'Oh yeah, sorry.' Cosmo shakes his head. 'I've been looking forward to Paris for ages.'

'Yeah, I know. But I didn't realise it's Leon's mum and dad's anniversary. They're having a big party.'

Great, Cosmo thinks, *so he's bailing on me to play happy families with his boyfriend.*

'I'll make it up to you,' Joshua says. 'I promise.'

Cosmo is unsure how to respond. However much he's hurting, however much he's feeling crushed, he has to remember that Joshua is his boss – and that he actually gave him his job. Six months after they met, Joshua said that they were looking for a reporter at QueerAndNow – and Cosmo had been desperate to leave the website of the down-market tabloid paper for which he was working.

He still went through a formal interview process, one Joshua insisted he passed fairly. But Cosmo will never know for sure if he'd have been offered the job if he and Joshua hadn't been seeing each other. And this gives him a sense of guilt that he can't shake. What he did went against all his principles.

Mind you, he thinks, *so does hiding my relationship away from my workmates, as if it's some kind of dirty secret.*

It's almost as bad as going out with someone in the closet – someone so ashamed of who they are that they hide away their true self.

Cosmo can't deny it any longer. There's no point pretending any more. This kind of set-up was never going to give him what he wanted. What he's looking for is a romantic relationship with a boyfriend he can take out with his friends and family – a boyfriend who makes him proud.

But what am I supposed to do about this gig up north? he wonders.

He'll just have to put his feelings to one side, along with his principles.

He clears his throat. 'That's OK. I understand.'

A smile sweeps across Joshua's face. 'Thanks, babe. Thanks for being pragmatic.'

Pragmatic? Cosmo thinks. *Really?*

He stands up. 'Look, I should probably get on with it. I need to book my train to Toddington.'

3

Cosmo is in a foul mood. He should have been heading off on a romantic weekend to Paris, but instead he's sitting on a much delayed, clapped-out train that's stuttering across the Pennine Hills.

As he gazes out of the window, he realises this is the furthest north he's ever been. He's struck by how beautiful the countryside is and how handsome the stone and red-brick buildings, although some of the town centres seem run down. He wonders if they might look more drab because the sky's the colour of slate.

He's distracted by two hairy men who are sitting opposite, swigging cans of lager.

'Here, what happened with that bird?' one of them asks his friend. 'Did you shag her or what?'

'Nah,' replies the other one, 'I think she was frigid.'

'Makes a change from the last one,' says his mate. 'She was a slag.'

Cosmo feels the bile leap into his throat.

He's about to demand the men stop being so disrespectful about women but stops himself. *What if they turn on me?* he thinks.

He suddenly feels conscious of his nail varnish and hides it under his sleeves. He also becomes aware of the colour of his skin. With one Indian grandparent and one Jewish, Cosmo is proud of his mixed background. *But there's no-one on this train who looks like me*, he notices.

A wave of fear passes through him. He shrinks back in his seat.

Tom slopes onto the pitch and tries to look keen. He's wearing rainbow-coloured laces woven through his boots and a rainbow armband around his right bicep. The other players jog on the spot, but he stays still.

Usually, Toddington's home stadium is his happy place. This is where he's felt the most joyful, the most passionate, the most *alive*. But today he just feels nervous. *What if this journalist can tell I'm gay?* he thinks.

It's a mild March day but clouds the colour of coal are rolling in from the hills. As the journalist is delayed and everyone wants to avoid being caught in a storm, the photographer starts taking pictures. As Tom holds his rainbow laces up to the camera, his heart thumps against his ribcage. *God, I feel like such a phoney*, he thinks.

Yes, in an ideal world Tom would like to come out of the closet. And he knows society is much more accepting of gay people than it used to be. The problem is, things haven't progressed so much in football; it's still a macho, old-school male world.

He looks at the empty seats around the stadium. Each week, Toddington's supporters roar as their team go into battle, hoping they'll win with a display of power, fitness and brute force. These aren't qualities many of them would expect from gay men – or at least the stereotype of a gay man. If Tom came out, he's worried he'd be rejected by the supporters – and the sponsors. *Not to mention the other players*, he tells himself. *What would Kyle say?*

Being the first footballer to come out would also make Tom a figurehead: it would put him in the position of having to overturn all these attitudes – and do it single-handedly. *I'm just not up to that*, he thinks.

He also remembers that his contract is coming up for renewal next season. *Now isn't the time to consider coming out*, he tells himself. *My agent would go ballistic.*

He does his best to stop working himself up into a tangle of stress.

He decides to pretend it's match day.

Right, he thinks, *game on!*

As he walks onto the grass, Cosmo imagines what the place must be like when the stadium is packed with fans. He can suddenly see why football stirs up such strong emotions – and surprises himself by feeling a little rush of excitement.

The club's publicist is called Jackie. She introduces him to a handful of players. There are a couple of midfielders, a charismatic striker called Uche – who even Cosmo recognises from adverts for sportswear and shaving products – and, at the end of the line, a well-built, pale-skinned man with ginger hair.

Cosmo feels a tingle run up his spine.

'This is our Tom,' says Jackie, with a warm smile.

Man, Cosmo thinks, *he's so hot I'd drink his bathwater.*

Not that Tom seems to have any awareness of his good looks. If anything, he seems shy and lacking in confidence. But Cosmo can't take his eyes off him; it's as if he's in some kind of trance.

Jackie coughs into her fist. 'Shall we make a start, flower?'

'Sorry, urm, yeah, let's do it.'

Cosmo takes out his voice recorder and asks the players how they feel about the Rainbow Laces campaign. Do they think football is becoming more accepting of minority groups? And what message are they hoping to send out by wearing the rainbow laces? He tries to involve all four players, but can't help directing most of his questions at Tom.

Before long, it becomes clear that the players are reeling off prepared statements that have been written by someone else. But if Cosmo's article is going to work, he needs them to speak more freely, to say something genuine.

He turns to Uche. 'Why do you think there are no openly gay players in the Premier League?'

Uche runs his hand along his undercut. 'I don't think it's because football's homophobic or anti-gay. It's more because it would be a lot for anyone to take on. You know, a lot of pressure.'

But somebody's got to do it – somebody's got to be brave enough! Cosmo wants to shout out.

'And how would you feel if one of your teammates came out?' he asks, calmly.

'I'd be proud,' Uche replies. 'It would be an honour to play beside him.'

That's more like it, Cosmo thinks. *That sounded genuine.*

He can't help noticing that Tom's kneading the back of his neck. *Why's he looking so tense?* he wonders.

He turns to face him. 'And what would you say to any gay players who are hiding in the closet? Any players who *want* to come out but are too frightened?'

Tom rocks backwards on his heels. 'Oh, urm, I don't know. It's not really . . .'

His words tail off.

Cosmo can feel himself getting fired up. 'Come on, if football's so accepting, wouldn't you tell him he's nothing to worry about? Or maybe to stop being a coward?'

Cosmo is shocked to hear the word coming out of his mouth; it's almost as if someone else has said it.

Uche steps forward. 'Mate, there's no need to be hostile. We're all doing our best.'

Jackie clicks her pen. 'Actually, I think that'll do. I'm sure you've got enough to work with.'

Tom feels a wave of anger lick his belly.

When he first saw Cosmo, he surprised himself by finding him attractive, with his sparkling green eyes, his playful smile and that edgy energy he gives off. And he admired the self-expression shown in his purple hair and nail varnish. But, after hearing him say the word 'coward', he felt under attack.

As he strides out into the car park, he spots Cosmo standing outside the main entrance, waiting for a taxi. Before he can talk himself out of it, he stalks over.

'Oi!' he calls out. 'You were a bit harsh!'

Cosmo swings round.

As their eyes meet, Tom feels his strong legs going soft. *Come on,* he tells himself, *snap out of it!*

'What you said was really out of order!' he barks.

Cosmo shakes his head. 'I'm sorry?'

'For a Premiership player to come out is a really big ask,' Tom says. 'Not everyone's built to be a leader.'

Cosmo seems taken aback.

Tom steams on. 'How can you be so insensitive? How can you not get it?' He pauses. 'Actually, don't answer that; you're just a typical journalist.'

Cosmo balls his hands into fists. 'Excuse me. I only challenged you because I *do* get it – I get just how difficult it is for queer kids.

20

I've seen enough of them struggling to accept themselves.'

'And what makes you think things would be any different for us?'

Cosmo's eyes swell.

Tom freezes. *Shit,* he thinks, *have I just given myself away?*

Cosmo's gaydar goes into overdrive.

Are you gay? he wants to ask. Then he realises he has.

Tom clutches at his neck. 'No, of course not.'

'Why "of course not"? Are you saying you can't be gay because you're too *masculine*?' Cosmo curls his lip. 'Typical footballer!'

Tom yells back, 'Just a minute, you don't know the first thing about me!'

In the distance, Cosmo hears a rumble of thunder. 'You know, if you are gay,' he powers on, 'if you came out, you could change the world!'

Tom exhales. 'Oh, give it a rest! I'm not gay and I'm not coming out!'

Cosmo's taxi swings into view just as the first drops of rain are falling.

Tom feels a judder of fear. *What if he goes back to London and starts spreading rumours?* he thinks. *What if I end up getting dragged out of the closet?*

His survival instinct kicks in. 'Get back to London and take your superior attitude with you!' he yells.

Cosmo yanks open the door. 'I'm going! I wouldn't want to stay in this bigoted backwater for a second longer!' He slams the door behind him.

As he watches the taxi drive away, Tom feels panic tightening his throat.

He thinks about his daughter, his dad, the club's fans.

Shit, he tells himself, *what have I done?*

4

In his bedroom in London, Cosmo taps on his keyboard.

When his story on the Rainbow Laces campaign was published, it didn't cause much of a stir. Whereas he knows that if he could break the story of the first ever Premier League player to come out as gay, that would kick-start a major moment in queer culture.

He's pretty sure Tom *is* gay . . . *But I couldn't force anyone to come out*, he thinks. *However much I might want him to.*

Instead, he's decided to write an opinion piece on why the Rainbow Laces campaign is all well and good but it's time for gay footballers to stand up and be counted.

'What are they so frightened of?' he types. 'The truth is, they're just pampered and cut off from real life. They only care about themselves and their sponsorship deals. But they need to realise they have a duty to their community!'

He pauses and lets out a breath. He imagines Tom reading the piece. *Will it inspire him to action or just wind him up even more?* he wonders.

He leans back and looks around the room. Stuck on the window are posters for Greenpeace and Amnesty International. On the wall hangs a copy of Keith Haring's painting for World AIDS Day. And next to his bed stands a photo of Cosmo as a teenager with his mum at a Lady Gaga concert – a concert during which his idol urged her fans to follow their dreams. He wonders what that idealistic boy would make of the man he's become. *I wonder what he'd think of my failure to make any mark on the world.*

He turns back to his computer but finds himself googling Tom Horrocks. He's surprised to discover that Tom has a seven-year-old daughter from a relationship with a woman. He wonders what the story behind that is. *Maybe he's right,* he thinks, *and I've misjudged how difficult it is for him.*

From downstairs comes the sound of his housemates giggling. Cosmo closes his laptop and takes a break.

For the last year, Cosmo has lived with Isabel, a bisexual friend he knows from school, and Ruby, a trans woman he met in the queue for vegan paella at the Mighty Hoopla festival. The three of them share a converted Victorian pub on the outskirts of East London – what they call their own little queer commune. Except the ground floor hasn't really been converted.

In fact, the main pub area remains as it was, but without the stock of booze. It's a big job for the three of them to clean it but at least the rent is cheap. They've plonked a TV on one of the tables, regularly use the pool table and dartboard, and do their best to keep the bar well stocked. And they still get a thrill from serving spirits by pushing up the little taps on the upside-down bottles.

Cosmo sees his friends sitting at a table in what used to be the snug. They're drinking a bottle of red wine and have already poured him a glass.

'What are you two giggling about?' he asks, pulling up a stool.

'That guy I went on a date with,' says Isabel, her russet-brown skin framed by the green tiles on the wall.

'Oh yeah, what's he done?'

Isabel rolls her eyes. 'The usual thing straight guys do when they find out I'm bi.'

'What, asked for a threesome?' says Cosmo.

Isabel cracks a smile. 'Yeah, but get this – with a man! I said, if you want to bring a dude into the bedroom, you might want to ask if *you're* bi!'

They laugh and Cosmo sips his wine. The discussion turns to Ruby and messages she's exchanged with an architect she's met on a dating app.

'He thought he was paying me a compliment when he told me I don't *look* trans,' she says, tossing her sleek brunette hair over her shoulder. 'Like, how am I supposed to respond to that?'

'You tell him where to get off,' quips Isabel.

'Don't worry, I did.' Ruby snickers. 'But he begged me for a date. He said he'd never been with a trans woman and it was on his bucket list.'

Cosmo and Isabel gasp.

'Honestly, I was livid. I said he'd have to find someone else to tick his box.'

In the background, the music playing on the jukebox changes to Cameo's 'Word Up'. As the pub closed in 1991, the selection of songs is stuck in the eighties – but that doesn't bother Cosmo, Isabel and Ruby, as it reminds them of the music their parents used to play.

'How about you?' Isabel asks Cosmo, fiddling with a curl from her Afro mohawk. 'What's happening with Josh?'

Ruby gives her a playful slap. 'Babes, you know you can't call him Josh!'

Isabel giggles. 'Sorry, Josh-*ua*.'

Cosmo tells them that he hasn't seen his boss outside work for nearly three weeks.

'You know, I've never bought that bullshit about him being in an open relationship,' comments Ruby, crossing her long, slim legs.

'Or if it is open, he's breaking the rules,' agrees Isabel.

The two of them repeat their advice to Cosmo to end the arrangement.

He lets out a sigh. 'I don't know, I just feel really sad about it. It was so exciting in the beginning. He made me feel so special. And I don't think I'm in love with him, but I do still care about him.'

'Fuck that!' erupts Isabel. 'Dump him and move on!'

'But it's not as simple as that,' Cosmo argues. 'He gave me my job, remember?'

'And?' says Ruby. 'You're really good at it!'

Cosmo runs his hands down his vintage corduroys. 'But what if he's vexed and makes things hard for me in the office?'

'Then you report him to HR,' suggests Ruby.

'What, and have people finding out how I got the job? Have the others thinking I got it because I was shagging the boss?'

Ruby wrinkles her nose. 'I didn't think of that.'

Cosmo runs a hand across his eyes. As he tops up their wine, he tells the girls that he'll just have to take his time and start planning his exit. He reminds them that his dream is to work for the *Guardian*; that would really give him the chance to make a difference. 'But for that to happen I'd have to nail a big story.'

'What have you got coming up?' asks Isabel, pulling at a stray thread on her shell suit.

Cosmo remembers an email he received just as he was leaving the office. He opens it on his phone.

He's been told to cover the Best of Britain Awards, which celebrate the UK's charity champions and unsung heroes. He'll be interviewing a music teacher who set up a choir for young queer people after her trans daughter took her own life.

Cosmo feels a rush of passion. *That's why I'm doing this job!* he thinks.

He tells this to the girls, then notices that the event is in Manchester, a city he's visited before and loves.

Something else catches his eye. 'I'll be coming too,' Joshua has written. 'So I'll book us a double room.'

Out of nowhere, Cosmo's sadness is swept away by a wave of hope. *Oh, maybe I should give our relationship another go*, he thinks. *Maybe this is a chance to get things back to how they were.*

Ruby quirks an eyebrow at him. 'Why are you suddenly looking so happy?'

'Oh, nothing, I'm just looking forward to the story, that's all.'

Eager to dodge any more questions, Cosmo opens the press release. He reads that some players from Toddington FC are going to be there. They will present an award to a man who runs a football club that brings together asylum seekers and local communities.

The image of Tom slams into his mind. In an instant, he remembers how attractive he found him, how he made his heart leap.

Is he going to be there? Cosmo wonders.

He shuts down his phone and picks up his wine.

5

At his home in Toddington, Tom is relaxing with a coffee he made using a machine that looks like a rocket engine. It was his latest find for a house he's equipped with the most advanced gadgets on the market. With modest needs, he often struggles to spend his money – so throws it at his already luxurious home.

It's a Sunday afternoon, the day after the Toddies won another game at home, and Tom's feeling excited about their winning streak.

As he hits a button to open the bifold doors that stretch across the back of the house, his phone pings. He picks it up to find a message from Uche, with a link attached.

'Have you seen this?' it reads. 'It's another article by that Cosmo.'

At the mention of Cosmo's name, Tom's body thrums with excitement. But, as he reads the article, once again he feels under attack.

'While the rest of society marches towards a more open, accepting future,' Cosmo writes, 'Premiership footballers are determined to let their so-called beautiful game fester in a dark, ugly past.'

Tom slams down his coffee cup. *Just what is his problem?* he thinks.

Outside, he hears a car crunching over the gravel driveway. He drops his phone on the sofa.

As soon as he's opened the door, his daughter Isla rushes over to hug him, her red hair tied up in a ponytail and pink lights flashing on the soles of her trainers.

'All right, pudding?' he says as he crouches down to give her a hug.

'Hiya, Daddy!'

As Isla charges into the house, Tom's ex-girlfriend Emily hands over her bags. 'Here you go,' she says with a scowl. 'She's been to a party so won't want her tea till later.'

'OK, thanks.'

'Oh and be warned; she's having a bit of a sugar rush.'

Tom forces out a chuckle. 'Noted.'

The silence curdles between them.

'How about you?' he asks. 'Are you all right?'

'Yep, fine.' Emily gives him a pinched expression and Tom feels his usual stab of guilt.

He'd only been seeing Emily for a few months when they found out they were expecting

Isla. Although Tom hadn't intended their relationship to be serious, he'd done what he thought was the decent thing and tried to make it work. In the end, though, that could never happen – so he'd finished the relationship when Isla was a toddler.

He'd known it would break Emily's heart but told himself it was the right thing to do; he felt terrible for lying to her, for using her to prove to himself that he could be 'normal'. That's why he'd put up with all the anger she threw at him, all her accusations that he was cold and afraid of opening himself up to love. That's why he still puts up with her hostility whenever he sees her – which is every few days, as they share custody of Isla.

'All right, well, enjoy the rest of your day,' he offers. 'See you on Wednesday.'

Emily nods, briskly. 'Bye, Isla!' she shouts over his shoulder.

From the kitchen, Isla calls, 'Bye, Mummy!'

Tom closes the door and goes over to his daughter. As he passes his phone, he thinks about Cosmo's article. *As if I could ever come out!* he tells himself. *Emily would rip me to shreds. She might even turn Isla against me . . .*

Sadness twists like a barb in his chest.

As soon as Isla's had some juice, she asks if

they can play rugby. Tom gives her a smile and pulls on a pair of trainers.

Once they're in the garden – on his enormous, springy lawn – the two of them practise passing and catching. After a while, Tom starts throwing the ball to Isla's side so she has to dive for it. When he notices a grass stain on her party dress, he worries Emily will use it as another reason to attack him. *I'll have to wash it before she goes back*, he thinks.

'So how was the party?' he asks. 'Did you have fun?'

Isla screws up her face. 'Not really. All the girls wanted to play dolls. They think I'm weird because I play rugby.'

Tom's heart slams into his throat. 'Well, don't you listen to them. You love rugby – you love getting muddy!'

She tilts her head. 'Yeah, but Sabina says it's a boys' game.'

'Isla, there's no such thing as a boys' or a girls' game! Look at football – people used to say that was a boys' game but now there's loads of girls who are brilliant at it.'

Isla squeezes the ball. 'I suppose so.'

'Anyway, you're unique, pudding. And don't you forget that!'

Isla sighs as she throws the ball back at him.

'Yeah, but Daddy, sometimes it's nice to be just like the others.'

Tom catches the ball and holds on to it. He isn't prepared for this conversation.

'Well, don't go changing for anyone,' he attempts. 'Daddy loves you just the way you are.'

God, you're such a fraud! he tells himself.

He wonders what Isla would say if she found out he's gay. *Come to think of it, would she even know what that means?*

He remembers taking her to his cousin's wedding last summer and her asking when he was going to find a new girlfriend.

No, I couldn't do that to her, he thinks. *I couldn't let her down.*

He drops the ball, lifts Isla in the air and whirls her around, making her squeal with delight.

'Come on,' says Tom, putting her down and kissing her on the head, 'shall we do some tackling?'

He knows that tackling always brings a smile to her face. At rugby training – where she's the only girl in a group of twenty – the kids aren't allowed to tackle until the age of nine. As Isla shoulder-barges Tom and he makes a big show of falling to the ground, he can't help thinking that she's at her happiest when she's lost in the game. In fact, she has the same passion for rugby as he had for football. As he still has for football.

His mind returns to the article written by Cosmo. *I need to ignore him*, he tells himself. *I need to remember the only reason I'm here is because of football.*

He vows once again to channel all his emotions into the game. *It's the only thing I've ever been good at,* he thinks, *the only thing I've ever got right.*

He thinks ahead to the next match, which is away in Manchester. When Isla goes inside to get a biscuit, he fetches his phone and messages Uche.

'Never mind that shitty article,' he types, 'am stoked for Saturday.'

'Totally!' comes the reply. 'With the right tactics, I reckon we can nail another win.'

Although Tom's happy to have moved the conversation on, he knows Uche will return to the article. He never shies away from difficult topics, which is how he got Tom to confide his sexuality. After repeatedly questioning why he showed no interest in women, Uche simply asked, 'Do you think you might be gay?'

There was something about the phrasing of the question, something about the compassion in his voice – not to mention the fact that the two of them were alone in the hotel room they share on away matches – that made Tom feel he had to answer. What followed was an intimate chat that left Tom feeling so relieved that he had to slip into the bathroom and have a little cry.

Uche adds, 'Oh and remember you're coming to those awards with me afterwards.'

'I'd forgotten about that,' types Tom. He feels a clutch of fear. 'I won't have to get up on stage, will I?'

'Mate, chill! I'm presenting an award. You're just my date.'

Tom remembers that he's filling in for Chanelta – Uche's influencer girlfriend – who's promoting a brand of lip gloss in Dubai.

'You know I've never dated a redhead before,' Uche teases. 'I hear they're wild in bed.'

Tom spots the chance for mischief. 'And I've never dated a black guy. But let's stay away from the clichés, shall we?'

Uche sends back several laughing emojis. 'Agreed! But you are still up for it?'

Tom thinks it might be their last chance to have some fun before the last run of games of the season.

'Yeah, count me in.'

6

Cosmo smooths down his seventies velvet suit and checks his reflection in the mirror.

He's in a suite in a swanky hotel in Manchester, where he's getting ready for the Best of Britain Awards. But he feels awkward in formal dress so takes off his tie and swaps his smart shoes for a pair of trainers. *That's much more me*, he thinks.

Not that he's looking forward to this evening. At the last minute, Joshua pulled out of the trip – explaining that his boyfriend's best friend was throwing a birthday party. Cosmo feels the sadness bloat inside him.

I'm just going to have to focus on the job, he tells himself. *I'll get an early night and catch the first train home tomorrow.*

In the same hotel, Tom and Uche are getting ready in their twin room. They're wearing outfits arranged by the club's media department – stylishly cut suits that have been specially made for them by a top menswear designer, finished off with bespoke ties in the club's famous purple.

As he sits down and laces up his shoes, Tom feels that familiar post-match ache in his muscles – but it's more than made up for by a strong dose of that familiar post-win high.

'Mate, I can't believe we beat Man U,' he chirps. 'And at Old Trafford!'

Uche looks in the mirror and adjusts his tie. 'I know, it's unreal.'

'Never mind the Champions League, maybe we could go all the way – maybe we could win the Premier League.'

'Well, that's what the journalists were saying.'

Tom blows out his cheeks. 'I don't know whether to be excited or terrified. Talk about pressure!'

Uche pats him on the back. 'Mate, don't think about any of that now – it's our night off. And they're going to be all over us on that red carpet!'

Cosmo scans the red carpet for Sue Tidewell. She's the award winner he interviewed this morning, but she was nervous about her speech so he wants to wish her good luck.

He can't see her. But he does spot a

nicotine-blonde drag queen called Labia Dribble, chatting to a posh designer with a diamond on her finger that's the size of a Brussels sprout.

Tom Horrocks strays into view.

Shit! he thinks. *So he is here!*

Cosmo considers hiding, but Tom's eyes clamp on to him – and he arrows him a hard look.

Despite the hostility, Cosmo can't help feeling a tickle in his heart. *Man, he's even more gorgeous than I remember!* he tells himself.

Tom strides over. 'Hi,' he says, gruffly.

'Hi.'

'I read that piece you wrote.' A sneer twists across Tom's face. 'You just won't give it a rest, will you?'

Cosmo thinks back to Sue's story, her trans daughter's suicide and the queer kids she mentors in her choir. 'I won't, no. Not until every queer kid in the country can feel proud of themselves.'

'And what?' says Tom. 'You don't care who you hurt in the process?'

'I didn't say that.'

Tom scoffs. 'No, I don't suppose it even crossed your mind.'

Cosmo is so shocked he can't help letting out a gasp. Then he rallies. 'Just a minute, what's it to you? You're straight, remember?'

Shit, he thinks, *did I really say that?*

Tom's cheeks stain the same red as the carpet. Without replying, he turns and stalks back to Uche.

Cosmo feels a spike of self-loathing.

He gives himself a telling off. *Man, you need to apologise!*

Over dinner in the ballroom – sitting at a table under a sparkling chandelier – Tom tips back his wine. Complete strangers approach him and Uche, asking for selfies and offering congratulations. It's a lot to take in, especially for someone who tries to keep a low profile.

Tom's also feeling shaken after seeing Cosmo. He didn't plan on starting an argument; the words just flew out of his mouth. And now he regrets them.

He goes for another swig of his wine but finds that his glass is empty. Before he can even call for a waiter, one has swept in and topped it up.

When the ceremony gets underway, Tom listens to moving and inspiring stories and applauds the awards.

'I'd like to dedicate this to my wonderfully queer daughter,' says a woman called Sue Tidewell, 'and to all the queer children who are still struggling to accept themselves. Remember, you are enough. You are *more* than enough!'

Her speech brings a tear to Tom's eye and he decides to make a big donation to her choir as soon as he's home. *That's what I can do with my money!* he thinks.

Before long, it's time for Uche to present his award – and he's given a standing ovation before he's even made it onto the stage. Tom watches with pride as he makes a stirring speech. But then Uche goes into the pressroom, leaving Tom alone with his wine.

By the time Uche slips back into his seat, Tom has progressed from tipsy to drunk.

'I just bumped into Cosmo,' Uche says.

'Really?'

'Yeah. He says he owes you an apology.'

'Well, he can stick it.'

Uche cocks his head. 'Mate, maybe you should give him a chance. He seems really taken with you.'

'What, like a snake's taken with a mouse?'

Tom excuses himself to go to the toilet – and heads outside to grab some air. As he's staggering across the lobby, he hears someone calling his name.

He spins around so fast that for a moment he feels dizzy.

He blinks and there's Cosmo.

'Look, before you say anything,' Cosmo starts, 'I just want to say I'm sorry. For what I said on the red carpet. It was totally out of order.'

Tom draws in a breath. He realises he isn't angry any more. *How can I be when he looks at me like that?* he thinks.

'That's OK,' he finds himself saying. 'Well, it's not, but . . . I get it.'

They hit a bump of silence.

Tom imagines leaning forward and kissing him. *Where did that come from?* he wonders.

'I don't suppose . . .' Cosmo tugs at his collar. 'I don't suppose you fancy a drink, do you?'

From a part of himself Tom hardly knew existed, he replies, 'OK, yeah.'

As they help themselves to wine at the post-show bar, Cosmo explains that he's done his follow-up interview with Sue, so he's now off duty.

'I'm here on my own,' he finds himself adding. 'I was supposed to come with this guy I've been seeing.'

Tom arches an eyebrow. 'Oh yeah?'

Wait a minute, thinks Cosmo, *why's he looking like that? Is he actually interested in me?*

42

'Oh, it's all very casual,' he says. 'And it's not going anywhere.'

Before he knows it, he's opening up and telling Tom the whole story. 'I mean, what if Joshua isn't in an open relationship and is cheating on his boyfriend? Where does that leave me and my principles?' He lets out a ragged sigh. 'Man, I'm such a fraud.'

Tom twists around one of his cufflinks. 'Don't say that. We're all stumbling through life. We all make mistakes. We're all just doing our best.'

Cosmo looks into his eyes and a flash of understanding passes between them. In that moment, he realises that Tom is much more sensitive than he'd thought. Then another thought occurs to him: *Maybe I was just prejudiced against footballers.*

'Yeah, I guess you're right,' he says.

Tom slides along the bar until there are only a few inches between them. Cosmo can't help noticing that he doesn't seem nervous about anyone seeing them together. *Mind you,* he thinks, *he's obviously pissed.*

Cosmo stops himself. *Wait a minute, maybe he's pissed* because *he's nervous.*

His heart swings open.

*   *   *

Once they've found a quiet corner in the hotel bar, Tom's surprised by how relaxed he feels. *But is that because of Cosmo?* he thinks. *Or is it because I'm wasted?*

Cosmo comes back to the table with what looks like two Cokes. 'I thought we'd move on to soft drinks,' he says, sitting down. 'I don't want you waking up and regretting bumping into me.'

Tom realises Cosmo is much softer – much more sensitive – than he'd thought. *It was wrong of me to think bad of all journalists*, he tells himself.

'Thanks,' he says, smiling. 'And don't worry, I won't regret it.'

Cosmo's eyes glitter. 'Good.'

There's a beat.

'Oh, and I *am* gay,' Tom blurts out, before he can stop himself.

It's as if his words reverberate around the space between them.

Cosmo nods, slowly. 'OK. Thanks for telling me.'

Tom tugs in a long breath. 'I wish I could tell everyone. But I can't.' And then it all comes tumbling out: the pressure from the club, the fans, worries about Isla, his dad . . .

'I have to say, that's a lot,' admits Cosmo. 'I'm

44

sorry again. I really wasn't very understanding. I guess I should be aware of my privilege.'

Tom's forehead creases. 'What do you mean?'

'Well, I've had an easy time with my family. And clearly, there's no conflict between my sexuality and my job; I've basically made a career out of being queer.'

Cosmo chuckles and Tom doesn't think he's ever looked so handsome.

I want to kiss you, he's on the verge of saying. He keeps it inside.

'That's a good thing,' he manages. 'You seem happy.'

A smile traces itself on Cosmo's face. 'Right now I am, yeah. Right now, here with you.'

Tom returns his grin. 'Me too.'

There's another beat. *Is this really happening?* Tom thinks.

His heartbeat is in his ears.

'I don't suppose you fancy coming to my room?' Cosmo asks.

Tom feels like he's reached the top of a rollercoaster and it's paused, waiting to plunge.

He lets out a breath he didn't realise he'd been holding. 'Yeah. I do.'

The two of them walk across the lobby. Although Cosmo continues chatting away,

Tom doesn't take anything in. He can feel the moisture draining from his mouth.

When the lift arrives, it's empty. As soon as the doors close, Tom grabs Cosmo. As their lips touch, an electric current shoots through him. His breathing becomes frenzied and his heart feels like it's going to burst out of his chest.

A bell sounds and Tom snaps back.

An old couple enter, arguing in some foreign language. They hardly notice Tom and Cosmo. But suddenly, Tom is aware of how they look to other people.

He hits the button for his floor.

'Sorry,' he splutters, 'I've got to go.'

'What?'

But Tom doesn't reply.

As soon as the lift arrives at his floor, he bolts.

7

For the next few days, Tom tries not to think about Cosmo. But he's worried that now he's let that part of him out, he won't be able to get it back in again.

On Tuesday afternoon, he takes his dad to a hospital appointment. Three years ago, Rod Horrocks was diagnosed with pancreatic cancer, and the tumour is wrapped around his aorta so it's impossible to remove. But, after a course of chemotherapy, it's at least stopped growing. The doctors have fitted Rod with a stent and, every six months, he has blood tests and a scan to check the cancer isn't active again.

Every six months, Tom is filled with terror as he waits to find out if his dad's been given another reprieve.

Doctor Cranfield, a middle-aged man with jet-black eyebrows and ghost-white hair, greets them outside his office.

'All right, doctor,' says Rod.

'Tom!' Doctor Cranfield bursts out, shaking

Rod's hand but barely registering him. 'How about Man U?'

As Tom and his dad sit down, the doctor launches into an analysis of Saturday's game, his eyes blazing. Tom's used to this kind of attention from men around Toddington – and, ordinarily, it's attention he can handle. But today, he just nods and agrees politely. *I wish he'd shut up and give us the test results*, he thinks.

The only reason Tom doesn't interrupt is because his dad is clearly enjoying the conversation; he's sitting taller and his face is aglow. 'I think Santos has got the shape of the team spot on,' he comments.

Tom manages a smile. When he was growing up, Rod was a robust, broad-beamed, imposing man, but these days he's smaller, diminished, fragile. One of the few things that lifts his spirits – one of the few things that seems to bring back anything like the vigour of his youth – is discussing the success of Toddington FC. Or, even better, watching them play. Watching Tom play.

'Wasn't our Tom belting?' Rod grins broadly. 'Did you see that tackle he made just before half time?'

Tom remembers that making his dad proud was one of the reasons he fell in love with football. When he was three years old, his mum walked out on the family, leaving Rod to bring up Tom single-handedly. Over the next fifteen years, Tom watched as his dad put his own life on hold, giving up everything for him. Tom didn't want to seem ungrateful, nor did he want his dad to think his sacrifice wasn't worth it. So he trained harder and harder, determined to play better and better. And the more he made his dad proud, the better he felt about himself.

Suddenly, he's hit by the memory of kissing Cosmo at the weekend. His heart plunges to his stomach.

Tom imagines what his dad would say if he knew he was gay. As a child, he used to hear Rod making awful comments about gay people. This was worse when he was around Tom's granddad, who often made fun of camp, effeminate men on TV – or told stories about some boy called George he remembered from school, a boy they'd nicknamed Georgina.

Tom hated hearing the two of them sneer. He hated knowing that what they were saying about other people was true of him. It aroused in him a self-disgust, a self-disgust he'd try and kick away on the football field.

No, he thinks, *I could never tell Dad I'm gay.*

Tom remembers how disappointed Rod had been when he and Emily had split up. His dad had always loved Emily, and hadn't understood why Tom had walked out on the relationship – just like his wife had walked out on him. That was the only time Tom had ever felt he'd let him down. And he'd sworn he wouldn't let him down again.

Besides, he thinks, *there's no way I could do it now he's ill . . .*

When a gap opens up in the conversation, Tom inches his chair forwards. 'So come on, what's the latest?'

Oh, please tell us the cancer's not growing, Tom thinks, screwing his hands into fists. *If you say that I'll do everything I can to force the gay back in again.*

Doctor Cranfield runs a finger over his eyebrow and consults his notes on his computer screen.

'I'm sorry,' he says after a while, 'but the scan does show there's been some growth in the tumour. And that's backed up by the blood tests.'

Tom feels as if a six-foot striker has just slammed into him.

The doctor starts talking about next steps, about palliative care, end-of-life treatment, the danger of catching an infection . . .

But Tom doesn't hear any of it. All he can think is, *This is your fault.* You *did this!*

8

Cosmo studies the menu in a crowded, painfully cool restaurant in Dalston. He's on a date with Joshua – and he's determined it'll be his last.

'I'm having the spatchcock chicken,' Joshua decides, tossing his menu onto the table. 'What are the veggie options like?'

'I'll probably just have the baba ganoush with pita,' Cosmo says. 'I'm actually not that hungry.'

More to the point, he thinks, *I feel sick knowing what I've got to do . . .*

While Cosmo was in Manchester, Isabel and Ruby went to a house party at which they recognised Joshua. After a few drinks, they managed to chat to his boyfriend, Leon. After some digging, they found out that Leon isn't in an open relationship at all – or at least he doesn't think so. Which means Joshua must be cheating on him.

And yes, Cosmo's aware that he's spent a lot of time since he's been back from Manchester thinking about Tom. He's spent a lot of time revisiting the intense attraction that buzzed between them – and how incredible it felt when they kissed. But he's no idea if their connection can develop into anything more meaningful. *How can it when my number one rule is not to date anyone in the closet?* he thinks.

He puts down his menu.

Right, stop getting distracted, he tells himself. *You need to end this with Joshua . . .*

A waitress with a bolt through her nose comes over to take their order. Once she's gone, Joshua pours two glasses of wine.

Cosmo takes one sip and can't hold himself back any longer. 'I know you're not in an open relationship,' he states. 'And I'm really unhappy about it.'

Joshua raises his eyebrows. 'Babe, what are you talking about? You know I wanted to keep things casual.'

'Yeah, but you said Leon was cool with it. You said you weren't breaking any rules.'

Joshua runs his hand over his beard. 'Look, I don't know why we're even having this conversation. Relationships are complex, you know that.'

Cosmo feels fire in the pit of his stomach. 'Are they? Are they really? Because I would have thought whether you're exclusive or not is actually quite simple.'

Joshua's face thickens. 'Cosmo, it's not my fault you wanted more than I could give.'

'That's not what's going on, Josh!'

'*Don't* call me Josh!'

It's like a whip has been cracked in Cosmo's head. 'Josh-*ua*, I'm not doing this any more. I'm not seeing you again.'

At the next table, a skinny woman holding a dachshund breaks into laughter.

Joshua arrows him a murderous look. 'Well, that's charming. You know I only gave you that job so we could mess around.'

Cosmo recoils. 'But you said I passed my interview fair and square.'

Joshua pretends to choke on his wine. 'Babe, I only said that so you'd stop all your whining. Although now I wonder if that was just part of your plan.'

'What's that supposed to mean?'

A thick vein pulses on Joshua's forehead. 'You used me, Cosmo. You used me to get what you wanted.'

'Joshua, that is not true!'

'Baba ganoush?' asks the waitress, reappearing between them.

Cosmo gives his head a shake. 'Sorry, that's me.'

She puts down both plates and leaves.

Cosmo stares at his food, then pushes it away. 'If that's what you think about me, Joshua, I don't think there's any point sticking around.'

He pulls on his coat and digs around the pockets for some cash.

'You know this is going to make things difficult at work,' Joshua says, his nostrils flaring.

Cosmo tosses a few banknotes onto the table. 'I was hoping we could be adults about it.'

'You'll regret this!' Joshua shouts after him as he stomps away.

Once he's out in the street, Cosmo continues stomping towards the bus stop. For every step he takes, his heart beats twice.

Thank fuck I've done that! he thinks.

Gradually, his anger gives way to relief.

But very soon this is overwhelmed by a cold slick of dread. *What's Joshua going to be like in the office?*

Cosmo reassures himself that he's done the right thing, whatever happens next.

Then, as he reaches the bus stop, his thoughts switch to Tom. *Oh, I know I keep telling myself that the one's got nothing to do with the other, but I'm actually not sure that's true . . .*

Now he's free of Joshua, Cosmo feels compelled to discover if there really could be anything between him and Tom.

But how could I even get hold of him? he wonders.

He's already checked social media and Tom has no presence at all.

Then another thought occurs to him.

Cosmo remembers the club's publicist inviting him back to watch a match. *Which was very nice of her,* he reflects, *considering I basically tore into the players.*

As he spots a bus approaching, he decides to take her up on the offer.

9

'Well, it's nice to see you, flower,' Jackie says to Cosmo. 'But if you don't mind me saying, it was a little unexpected.'

The two of them are sitting in the pressroom of Toddington FC's home stadium, which is stuffed full of sports journalists. It's at the end of a line of posh boxes, which have waiter service for champagne, a buffet of chef-prepared food, and rows of padded seats outside. Cosmo hadn't known football could be so glamorous.

'Yeah, sorry,' he replies, 'I did get a bit carried away. I've got over myself now.'

'Good to hear it.' Jackie tucks her blonde hair behind her ear. 'Out of interest, what was it that made you want to come back?'

Cosmo picks up his match programme and turns it around in his hands. 'Oh, I just fancied getting away from London.'

Jackie raises an eyebrow. 'What is it, man trouble?'

'Something like that.' The truth is, Cosmo's been having a hard time at work, with Joshua finding fault with whatever he does – but he doesn't want to tell Jackie that he used to sleep with his boss. And he can hardly tell her that he made the journey especially to see if there could be anything between him and Tom. 'You know what it's like,' he says, waving his hand, vaguely.

Jackie gives a wry smile. 'I do, flower. I spend every day surrounded by fellas – I know *just* what they're like!'

They laugh.

Their chat is ended by a voice coming from the loudspeaker, followed by a roar from the crowd.

Cosmo darts over to a space by the window, just in time to catch the players trotting onto the pitch.

The whistle blows and Tom moves to mark his opponent. When a striker from Wolverhampton Wanderers passes the ball to his teammate, Tom intercepts it and slides a pass out wide to Kyle.

As his boots bounce along the grass, the adrenaline spikes through him and his heart pounds. It's as if he's become a machine rather than a man – a perfectly tuned, high-performance machine.

When Toddington win a corner, Tom moves up the pitch and flicks a header to Uche, who slams it into the back of the net.

An intense joy crashes into Tom. The shouting and stomping from the stands is so loud that his arms break into goosebumps. He and his teammates hug each other and leap up, punching the air.

This is what it's all about! he thinks. *This is who I am!*

And they're off again.

Although the fans continue to cheer and chant, Tom doesn't even look up. Once again, he's laser-focused on the game.

Nothing else matters. Nothing else can bother him.

He's lost in football.

Cosmo walks down the stairs and into the throng. It's half time and he wants to experience what match day is like for the fans.

He might as well have travelled a million miles from the pressroom. As he strolls around, he passes betting stalls, bars serving beer in plastic glasses, and TV screens showing results from across the Premier League.

So far, the Toddington game has been evenly

matched, but the home team have the edge and are winning 1–0. Although Cosmo only just caught Uche's goal; he found it difficult to take his eyes off Tom. Even from a distance, the pull of his good looks was impossible to resist.

Cosmo feels a surge of excitement. *I'll be seeing him later*, he thinks.

He felt guilty as he'd told Jackie that he'd chatted to Tom at the Best of Britain Awards and had promised to pop down and say hello after the game. *Oh, I know that isn't strictly true,* he thinks, *but it would have been if Tom hadn't run off as soon as we'd kissed.*

The memory of his panicked escape hits Cosmo like a punch to the gut. *What's he going to say when he sees me?* he wonders.

Jackie mentioned that she'd be going down to supervise the media interviews and Cosmo was welcome to tag along, an offer he instantly accepted. But now he isn't so sure it's a good plan. He thinks it might be unfair to just spring himself on Tom.

Cosmo approaches a stall and orders a cheese and onion pie with mushy peas. As he bites into it – surprised at how good it tastes – he spots a gay couple, wearing rainbow pins on their jackets and openly showing each other affection. No-one takes any notice.

He realises just how wrong he's been about Toddington: *I basically saw two dickheads on the train and got scared the whole town was like that.*

He feels a stab of shame.

At least he's repainted his nails and re-dyed the tips of his hair purple, to signal his support for the Toddies. *I hope Tom likes it*, he thinks.

Tension tightens in his stomach.

He notices people starting to return to their seats. It's time to go back for the second half.

Once the match is over and Tom emerges from the dressing room, his eyes land on Cosmo.

Fear cuts through him.

But at the same time, his spirit soars.

What does that mean? he wonders.

'All right, Tom?' says Jackie. 'Well played, lad.'

'Thanks, Jack.'

'Now, I've got to shoot off.' She nods towards Cosmo. 'Can I leave this one with you?'

As Cosmo waits for Tom to answer, Tom sees the worry on his face. *Shit,* he thinks, *what do I say?*

Tom knows what he *wants* to say. But he thinks about his dad, who texted him to say he was watching from his usual seat. He thinks about his vow to force his gayness back inside.

I can't, though, he tells himself. *I just can't. This thing's stronger than me.*

He sucks in a breath.

'Yeah,' he says.

A smile washes over Cosmo's face.

'Ta-ra then!' chirps Jackie, and she bounds off down the corridor.

Tom and Cosmo's eyes fix onto each other's and there's a tense pause. A physio walks past and waves goodbye at Tom.

Tom guides Cosmo into the tunnel, where it's quieter. 'So did you enjoy it?' he asks.

'Yeah!' Cosmo says. 'And I don't know much about football but I could see you played brilliantly. Especially when you headed the ball halfway across the pitch!'

Tom shrugs. 'Oh, you know, I was just doing my job.'

'It's more than a job,' Cosmo insists. 'It's a superpower!'

Tom laughs. There's another pause, and he shifts his weight from one foot to the other. He remembers what happened the last time he saw Cosmo.

'Your hair's nice,' he blurts out. 'Did you dye it again?'

Cosmo reaches up and touches the tips. 'Yeah, I wanted it to stand out for the game. And I did my nails.' He holds out his hand.

'You did that for us?' says Tom.

Cosmo's smile crawls into his eyes. 'Well, for you.'

Tom's stomach flips.

'So what happens now?' asks Cosmo. 'Do you all go out?'

Tom frowns. 'No, it's very low-key. What you saw last week was a one-off.'

The memory of him bolting out of the lift rises up like a barrier between them.

'Look, about last week,' he says, 'I'm really sorry. I just found it a bit . . .'

'It's OK,' chips in Cosmo, 'I get it. I get it even more after today. But let's not talk about that. Let's just focus on your win.'

Tom runs his hand up and down the strap of his bag. 'OK, well . . .' He screws up all his courage. 'We can celebrate together if you like?'

A few hours later, Tom arrives at Cosmo's Airbnb, holding a bottle of wine and a bag of takeaway food.

As he sets eyes on him, Cosmo's pulse trips. He isn't sure how to greet him but doesn't have to decide as Tom's hands are full. Cosmo gestures for him to come through to the kitchen.

'This is a nice place,' Tom comments.

Cosmo is staying in a flat on Toddington's rather forlorn-looking high street, above a men's clothes shop called Klobber. It's decorated in neutral colours and the furniture is bland, but the owner has at least left a vase of freshly picked bluebells on the table.

Next to it, Tom places the wine and food. 'I'm treating you to what up here we call a chippy tea.'

Cosmo rubs his hands together. 'I can't wait!'

The first parcel Tom opens turns out to be his: rag pudding with chips and gravy. 'I normally have to watch what I eat but I'm having a cheat night,' he explains, then breaks into a grin. 'I want to show you the best Toddington has to offer.'

Cosmo grins back at him. 'Thanks so much.'

Tom unwraps the second parcel, revealing a vegetarian sausage with chips and mushy peas. 'This is yours.'

Cosmo gives a little squeak. 'Oh, mushy peas, I had them earlier!'

Tom's face falls. 'Sorry, I didn't realise.'

'No, don't apologise,' insists Cosmo, grabbing some cutlery. 'I love them! And I didn't have chips; I've always wanted to taste proper northern chips.'

Tom pulls out a chair. 'Well, I promise that isn't all we eat.'

'I'm sure it isn't,' Cosmo says. He can't resist adding, 'You don't get legs like that from eating chips.'

Tom gives him a playful swat. 'Hey, you shouldn't be looking at my legs. You're seeing someone, remember?'

Cosmo narrows his eyes. 'No, I'm not. Not any more.'

The air between them crackles.

'Come on,' says Tom, 'let's tuck in before it gets cold.'

Tom takes a sip of his wine. They've moved from the kitchen to the sofa in the living room. They've been getting on brilliantly and have hardly stopped talking – about their lives, their upbringings, their passions.

Cosmo is telling Tom about the book he wants to write. It's called *How to Be an Activist Every Day* and is packed full of practical tips, from refusing plastic bags in corner shops to turning the temperature down on the washing machine. His conviction is infectious and Tom can't help feeling inspired. He's so engrossed that not for one second does he think about his dad. Not for one second does he think about Toddington's supporters. In this little flat, he and Cosmo are cut off from the rest of the world. He feels safe. He feels free.

'You know you're very sexy when you get passionate,' he says.

'Really?' replies Cosmo. Then he smirks. 'You're very sexy when you play football.'

'Thanks.'

There's another crackle between them.

Tom can't resist any longer. He puts down his wine and moves in to kiss Cosmo. *And this time I'm going to do it properly*, he thinks.

He pulls Cosmo closer and soon their breath is quickening and their kisses becoming frenzied.

Tom breaks away and stands up. He holds out his hand.

'Come on, we're going to your bedroom.'

10

Tom is in London, preparing for a game against Arsenal. He's nervous but excited, as Arsenal are just one point ahead of Toddington at the top of the League. Beating them would give the Toddies a clear chance of ending the season in first place.

He's equally nervous and excited about seeing Cosmo after the game. Their date has been on his mind all morning – as he and the team went for their walk around the hotel, ate their pre-match meal, and did their warm-up. It's still on his mind as he sits in the dressing room waiting for the referee to press the bell, calling them onto the pitch.

Last weekend, he and Cosmo had a wonderful night together – and it didn't end there. The next morning, Tom drove them up to the moors and they went for a long walk, which was every bit as wonderful. After he'd dropped Cosmo at the station, Tom couldn't stop smiling.

But now he just feels panicked and unsure of himself. *And that's not ideal on match day*, he thinks.

'What's up, mate?' asks Uche.

Tom snaps out of his daze. 'Oh nothing, don't worry. I'll be all right once I'm out there.'

Around the dressing room, the players are stretching out their muscles.

Kyle lets out a roar. 'Come on, lads! Let's switch into beast mode!'

Tom hears the bell press and springs up.

And into his head burst two words: *Game on!*

Cosmo leans back on the sofa and puts his feet up.

He isn't watching the match from the stadium as he doesn't want his housemates to question his sudden interest in football – it was bad enough lying to them when he went up to Toddington last weekend. So, knowing his dad supports Arsenal and subscribes to the sports channels, he's timed a family visit to coincide with the game.

'Well, this is nice,' says Joel Roberts, a bald man with a kindly face. 'I don't think you and I have ever watched the footie together.'

Cosmo smiles. 'You always said we should be open to all influences.'

Joel and Laura Roberts are proud of giving their children a liberal, open-minded upbringing. As well as instilling them with a respect for their own background, they also taught them to respect cultures other than their own. So the family living room is stuffed full of books about race and the legacy of Empire, plus trinkets, wall hangings and tribal masks collected from around the world.

As usual, the latest issue of the *Guardian* lies on the coffee table. On the front page is a photo of a march by striking teachers. From an early age, Cosmo's parents took him on protests and taught him to stand up for what's right.

'Where's Mum?' he asks.

'She's started volunteering at the food bank on Saturdays,' Joel replies. 'I think she likes to keep out of my way while I'm watching the footie.'

They return to the match and Joel adds to the commentary by offering his own insights into Arsenal's form.

'I know they're my team but if we're going to lose to anyone, I wouldn't mind it being the Toddies,' he confesses. 'What they've done this season has been nothing short of astonishing.'

In the end, Arsenal don't lose; they beat Toddington 2–0. And in Cosmo's inexpert opinion, Tom doesn't play well.

Man, I hope he isn't down about it, he thinks. *I hope it doesn't spoil our evening.*

Although they had a great time together on their last date, Cosmo reminds himself to tread carefully. *I don't want to come on too strong and scare him off.*

He texts Tom to offer his sympathy and to give him the details for the restaurant he's chosen.

As he realises this is their first date in public, unease shifts in his chest.

As Tom sits in a taxi on his way to Kentish Town, in his head he replays the post-match dressing-down Sergio gave the team, insisting they mustn't lose focus at this crucial stage. And he replays the phone call with his agent in which he was advised not to drink till the end of the season – and to block out all distractions. He wonders if Cosmo classes as a distraction.

When he arrives at the restaurant, Tom discovers that it's vegan, gluten-free *and* carbon neutral. The furniture looks like it's been sourced from the local dump. The chalkboard menu includes various items that claim to be 'artisanal' or 'foraged' – words Tom isn't sure he even understands. And he seems to be the only customer who doesn't have a moustache or a mullet.

Cosmo waves at him from the table. As Tom notices a diamante pendant hanging around his neck, he suddenly realises how obvious it is that he's gay. *Will everyone be able to tell we're on a date?* he worries.

Then he feels a stab of self-loathing.

He wishes they were back in Cosmo's Airbnb.

He isn't sure how to greet Cosmo and settles on a hug. But he's stiff and can't relax. *God, I'd kill for a drink*, he thinks.

He sits down and they chat through the game.

'A loss is gutting,' Tom admits, 'but it doesn't mean we can't still win the League.'

'Oh no?' Cosmo takes a pull on his craft beer.

'It just means Arsenal are four points clear,' Tom replies. 'So we have to win every match from now on – and they have to lose.'

He can't help glancing around to check he doesn't know anyone. He pours some water into a thick glass that reminds him of the ones they had at school dinners.

A waiter wearing a flat cap approaches their table. Tom's about to say that where he's from it's only old men who wear flat caps – and never indoors. But he stops himself.

Once they've ordered, Tom sits back and sips his water.

'So did you say your mum lives in London?' Cosmo asks, brightly.

Tom bristles. 'Yeah, I think so.'

'When was the last time you saw her?'

'I've told you,' Tom replies, surprised at how stern he sounds. 'When I was three.'

Cosmo swallows. 'And do you never get tempted to look her up?'

'No.'

Why would I want to look up a woman who dumped me as if I meant nothing? Tom thinks. He folds his arms to signal that the subject's closed.

He feels a rumble of guilt as he remembers how open he and Cosmo were with each other last weekend. 'Sorry,' he offers, 'I'm just not a big fan of London.'

A shadow passes across Cosmo's face.

The best thing in London is you, Tom wants to say. But for some reason the words won't come out.

'I suppose it just seems big and impersonal to someone like me,' he manages.

'I guess it's different for those of us who grew up here,' Cosmo says.

The silence grows thick between them.

Cosmo fiddles with his pendant. 'Have you ever brought Isla here?'

Isla? Tom thinks. *What's she got to do with it?*

'I haven't, no,' Tom answers, more angrily than he intended.

Cosmo drains his beer. 'From what you said last weekend, she sounds like a great girl. I'd love to meet her.'

Every muscle in Tom's body clenches. *Why do I feel like I'm under attack?*

When the waiter brings their food, he realises they've messed up his order, but he doesn't have the confidence to point it out. *What is this place?* he thinks. *What am I even doing here?*

After they've eaten their main course, Cosmo finds the conversation a slog.

He tells himself that it's his fault for asking Tom such personal questions, for being unable to switch off his inner journalist. *It's different now we're out in public*, he thinks. *He probably feels exposed.*

'Hey, Cosmo!' calls out a high-pitched voice.

He looks up to see a loud, theatrical friend approaching their table.

Oh God, he thinks. *This is all we need . . .*

Cosmo stands up and gives his friend a stiff hug. 'K, this is Tom. Tom, this is K.'

Tom's forehead puckers. 'K? As in the letter?'

K smiles. 'Yeah, it's my chosen name.'

'Ah, all right,' Tom says. 'So how do you boys know each other?'

K gives a sharp gasp.

'K's actually non-binary,' Cosmo explains, hoping he doesn't sound patronising.

'Don't worry, people misgender me all the time,' K says, smiling.

Tom, on the other hand, looks embarrassed and miserable.

'Wait a minute,' K bursts out, almost screeching, 'I *know* you!'

Tom frowns. 'Really?'

K's hands flap excitedly, attracting the attention of the people on the surrounding tables. *Man,* Cosmo thinks, *can this get any worse?*

'You play for Toddington!' K cheeps. 'That's where *I'm* from!'

Tom nods and K squeals so loudly that Cosmo can't help wincing.

'Hold on,' K says, 'is this a date..? Are you . . .?'

Tom blushes to the tips of his ears.

'Don't be daft!' Cosmo sing-songs. 'We met through work and I'm giving Tom advice about joining social media. He's got to be the only footballer in the world who isn't on Instagram!'

K gives another gasp and the waiter interrupts with their desserts.

'Well, I'll leave you to it,' K says, kissing them both before flouncing out.

When Cosmo and Tom are left on their own, something has shifted.

Cosmo feels guilty for being ashamed of K. He feels even worse for concealing another gay man's sexuality.

He signals to the waiter that he wants another beer.

This is why I can't date someone in the closet. He realises he's shared his thought out loud.

'That's fine,' Tom says, fire flashing in his eyes, 'because I'm not ready to come out. So at least we know where we stand.'

Cosmo nods, firmly.

They've hit a dead end.

And, without anything being said, Cosmo knows Tom won't be inviting him back to his hotel.

11

Cosmo is gutted. Since their disastrous date in London, Tom has ignored his messages or sent short, sometimes curt replies.

There's nothing else for it: he tries to cast Tom out of his mind.

So far, his strategy has been to focus on work. But that only makes him feel worse.

'I'm sure Joshua's started seeing one of the other reporters,' he tells Isabel and Ruby.

It's a Tuesday night and the three of them are enjoying one of their regular sessions of pub games.

'And? What's the problem?' says Isabel, throwing her third dart at the worn-out board.

'Oh, I'm not bothered about it on a personal level,' Cosmo says. 'Only professionally. Joshua's giving him all the best stories and tossing me the scraps. I'm finding it hard to do a good job.'

Isabel pulls out her darts and chalks up her score. 'I reckon that could be your cue to leave, mate.'

'Yeah,' says Cosmo. 'I probably need to bring my job search forward.'

Ruby stands on the line and aims her first dart. 'More importantly, now you're free of the dickhead, we need to set you up with a new profile on Hinge.'

Cosmo wriggles on his stool. 'Oh, I don't know . . .'

As she hits a score of ninety, Ruby gives a little shimmy. 'Why not, babes? You're ready to move on.'

Dare I tell them? he thinks.

Cosmo rubs his face with the heel of his hand. 'The thing is, I *have* started to move on.'

The girls turn to face him. After swearing them to secrecy, Cosmo tells them about Tom. They suspend their game and sink onto stools, both of them transfixed.

'Look, I'm sorry I didn't tell you earlier,' Cosmo says. 'But he didn't want anyone to know. He isn't ready to come out.'

Isabel and Ruby exchange a worried look.

'I know what you're going to say,' Cosmo says, 'but he's a bit of me and I really like him. Man, I don't know what to do.'

Isabel shakes her head, her hoop earrings catching on her shoulders. 'I'm sorry, but you have to stick to your policy of not getting involved with anyone in the closet.'

'But what if he can't come out now but will do eventually?'

Ruby runs her long, pink nails through her newly conditioned hair. 'I do get that it's hard for him. And I get that you want to cut him some slack.'

'But if Tom does decide to come out,' Isabel says with a stern look, 'he has to do it for himself, not you. It'd put the relationship under too much pressure.'

'You wouldn't want him to end up resenting you, babes,' adds Ruby, squeezing his knee.

Cosmo nods, slowly. He knows they're right. *But I've never felt like this before*, a voice inside him protests. *How am I supposed to let it go?*

'Come on,' he says, standing up and grabbing his darts, 'it's my go.'

Tom's trying not to think about Cosmo and to stay focused on football.

It's the day after a midweek match and Sergio is leading the players through a video analysis. While Toddington won 3–1, Arsenal suffered a surprising loss, which has kept alive the

Toddies' dream of winning the Premier League. As he listens to the manager outline his latest plan, Tom tells himself that he's doing the right thing: he has to force back his feelings.

After training, he picks up Isla from school. As soon as they're home, she asks if they can play rugby. But her teacher told him that she has some homework so Tom insists on doing that first.

They sit on two stools at the island in Tom's shiny, designer kitchen, and Isla tells him she has to draw a picture of someone who inspires her. 'It's for our Hall of Heroes.'

Tom leans forward. 'OK, and who are you going to do?'

Isla takes out a pad of paper and a pencil case. 'The two boyfriends who came to talk to us for LGBT History Month.'

The shock of it stops Tom's breath. *What?* he thinks. *How did I not know about this?*

In an instant, his heart is racing but he manages to ask, softly, 'What do you mean, two boyfriends?'

Isla rolls her eyes. 'Daddy! Two boys can love each other, you know. They're called gays.'

Tom seizes a breath and waits for his insides to settle. 'Yes, I do know that, pudding. I just wasn't sure you did.' He clears his throat. 'And what were their names, these gays?'

Isla looks down and begins sketching. 'Albert and George. They fell in love when they were young, but they had to break up because people used to be horrible to gays. Then, when Albert got old, he went looking for George and found him. And now they've fallen in love again.'

Tom feels an ache in his gut. 'Well, that's a lovely story.'

'Albert said you should never be afraid of your difference because it's what makes you special,' says Isla, nodding and giving her pigtails a bounce.

Tom looks down and sees that she's drawn a picture of two men kissing, surrounded by a love heart. Tears well in his eyes.

'And he's right!' he bursts out. 'You need to remember that next time anyone calls you names for playing rugby!'

Isla opens a pack of felt-tip pens and begins colouring in her drawing. 'He also said you can only be happy when you're being true to yourself.'

Tom feels a tear escape and run down his left cheek. 'That's very wise, Isla. I can see why Albert's your hero.'

Not wanting Isla to see him upset, he goes over to the sink and knuckles away the tears. He pours himself a glass of water but, rather than drinking it, just stands there, staring at the wall.

So if I came out of the closet, I wouldn't lose Isla, he realises. *I might even inspire her.*

He lets out a wobbly breath as he repeats to himself, *'You can only be happy when you're being true to yourself.'*

In that moment, it hits him that if he's ever going to be happy – really, truly happy, not just suppressing his scary, negative feelings – he needs to accept his sexuality. *I need to come out,* he thinks.

He picks up the phone and texts Cosmo.

12

After taking a week off work to apply for new jobs – including a reporter role that's become vacant at the *Guardian* – Cosmo travels to Toddington for a long weekend. It's a trip he's hoping will change everything.

Last week, Tom called him to say he was ready to come out of the closet. Cosmo was so shocked – and so elated – he hardly knew how to respond. But Tom said he was already making a plan and just needed his help.

As Cosmo booked his train and the same Airbnb in which he'd stayed on his last visit, he tried to rein in his excitement. *Remember, this is going to be a massive life change for Tom*, he tells himself. *You need to be sure he can cope.*

Tom collects Cosmo from the station and, rather than driving him to the Airbnb, suggests they go for another walk on the moors. They park outside a big Tudor manor house called Toddington Hall, and Tom pulls out two pairs of walking boots.

'I remembered we're the same size,' he says.

'Very impressive,' quips Cosmo.

Tom pulls his laces tight. 'I'm taking you on a route we call going "over the tops".'

Cosmo gives a wry smile. 'You know me, I'm happy with anything over the top.'

As the two of them giggle, Cosmo feels a swell of relief. He realises he's been carrying a lot of tension. And it won't go away till he's heard about this plan.

They set off walking and Tom leads them across a railway bridge and up a gravel footpath, past run-down farm buildings and patches of woodland dotted with bluebells. Eventually they emerge at the bottom of a hillside. As they climb, the moors open up around them, into a moving mass of luscious greens and long, golden grasses.

'Man, this is beautiful!' Cosmo gushes. 'I can see why they call it God's Own Country.'

'Actually, that's Yorkshire,' says Tom, 'but on behalf of Lancashire I'll take the compliment.'

When they come to a boundary stone, they stop and look out over the town. Tom points out the parish church and the town hall, but dominating the skyline is the huge football stadium. Cosmo suggests they pause and sit down.

'Tom, when you said you're ready to come out . . .' he begins. 'Are you absolutely sure?'

Tom gives an emphatic nod. 'Yeah. I'm dead set.'

Cosmo feels all the tension leaving his body.

Tom confides that his only worry is having to go on the pitch and play as the first openly gay footballer in the Premier League, knowing the world is watching. 'I just couldn't handle the pressure.'

'OK, I get that.' Cosmo pinches at the bridge of his nose. 'But how can you avoid it?'

As Tom picks at the grass, he outlines his plan. He wants to record an interview with Cosmo. It would go live on the QueerAndNow website once the final match of the season is underway, just after the team has gone back onto the pitch for the second half. 'So people will hear the news *during* the game.'

Cosmo cocks his head. 'But how will that help?'

Tom strips the seeds from a stem of grass. 'Once I'm on the pitch, I know I can block everything out. I know I can focus on the game.'

'And afterwards?'

'That's just it,' Tom says, becoming more animated. 'By the time I'd have to face anyone, I'd have done it; I'd already be the first openly gay footballer to play in the Premier League.'

'So you wouldn't have to go out there feeling the weight on your shoulders ...'

Tom tugs up another stem of grass. 'Exactly. I'd have proven a point before I even come off the pitch.'

Cosmo rubs his jaw. 'It'll still be tough, though. You'll still get a lot of attention and you'll need to be prepared for that. Does the club offer any mental health support?'

Tom says there's a very good team psychologist. 'But I don't want to consult her yet. She might not like my plan ... She might try to talk me out of it.'

'But do you promise you'll see her afterwards?'

Tom strips another stem of its seeds. 'I promise.' He throws the grass over the hillside. 'So what do you think? Will you do the interview?'

Cosmo cracks a smile. 'Of course I will. But on one condition.'

'What's that?'

'That we keep your coming out separate to whatever is happening between us. I don't want you to be doing this for me. I want you to do it for yourself.'

Tom tugs in a deep breath, then lets it out slowly. 'I *am* doing it for myself.'

'OK, in that case count me in,' chirps Cosmo.

'We can do the interview tomorrow; then I'll have plenty of time to write it up.'

'Brilliant.' Tom slides along the grass, closer to Cosmo. 'Now we've worked that out, can we park it?'

'What do you mean?'

A smile plays at the corners of Tom's mouth. 'Well, you said you wanted to keep my coming out separate from what's happening between us.'

'Yeah?'

'Well, now I'd like to focus on us.'

He leans in to kiss him.

13

A few weeks later, Tom's dad is admitted to hospital with sepsis – after shivering wildly and vomiting bile. Having been moved to a ward and connected to a drip that gives him antibiotics which, the doctor jokes, are stronger than Domestos, he's dozing peacefully. Thankfully, Tom has been able to get his dad a private room, which at the very least gives Rod a much quieter, calmer setting.

Sitting by his bedside, Tom feels ripped through with worry. First of all, he's terrified of losing his dad. But Rod's setback also calls into question his plan to come out. As there are just three days left till the final game of the season, he thinks he's going to have to postpone. *I've got to put Dad first*, he tells himself.

Then another voice in his head says, *But what about Cosmo?*

The two men had a brilliant weekend in Toddington and have been talking and texting every day since. *I couldn't bear to let him down*, he thinks.

He looks at his dad, wired up to machines and monitors, his skin tinged with yellow. *Then again,* he tells himself, *Cosmo will understand. He's the one who said we should keep me coming out separate from us.*

Then he remembers Cosmo's policy of never dating anyone in the closet. *Will he go back to that if I can't go through with it?* he wonders.

'A penny for them?'

Tom gives a start. 'Dad! I thought you were asleep.'

'Oh, I was just resting my eyes.'

Tom smiles. It's what his dad always says when he falls asleep watching TV at home.

'How are you feeling?' he asks.

Rod lets out a raspy breath. 'Jiggered, to be honest. But it'll take more than this blasted sepsis to finish me off.'

'That's the spirit!' Tom holds up a fist but isn't sure either of them is convinced.

Rod angles his body to face him. 'So come on then, what *were* you thinking?'

'Oh nothing. It's not important.'

Rod smooths out a crease in his crisp white bed sheet. 'Tom, I know you've been seeing someone.'

Tom's gut twists. 'You what?'

'Do you think I didn't notice you disappearing

the other weekend? And staying out last month!'

A crack in Tom's plastic chair starts digging into his back. He wriggles himself free. 'I suppose it was kind of obvious.'

Outside, somebody shouts down the corridor.

Rod's eyes stay on the door. 'I also know it's a fella,' he says.

The shock wipes Tom blank.

Rod turns to look at him. 'I think I've always known you're gay, son. Although for a long time I tried to deny it to myself.'

Tom's about to say sorry, but stops himself.

Rod goes on, 'I suppose when your mum left me I felt like a failure. And my dad – your granddad – used to tell me it was my fault for driving her away. It's no excuse, but I think I tried to act like the big man to make up for it. And that involved slagging off gays – or at least men who weren't very manly.'

Tom can see a shadow of remorse scud across Rod's face. He worries that the conversation might be causing him added pain. 'Yeah, but—'

'Yeah but nothing, Tom. I shouldn't have said those things. Not when I suspected the way you were.' He lets out a hoarse sigh. 'I guess I was just scared that, if you were gay, it would make me less of a man. It would make me even more of a failure.'

Tom sits forward. 'Dad, is this really the right time to be having this conversation?'

'Yeah, it is, son. Because if anything happens to me I don't want you thinking I disapproved – or didn't love you as you are.'

Tom blinks, several times. He's never heard his dad discuss his feelings before, let alone express his love for him.

'Oh, I know I'm getting soppy,' Rod says. 'But that's what happens when you're on your way out. And I am on my way out, Tom – sepsis or no sepsis.'

Another silence sets in. From the other side of the door comes the sound of high heels clicking down the corridor.

'One thing I've learned,' Rod continues, 'is that life's too short to be unhappy. And if you like this bloke – if you *love* him – you should go for it.'

Tom inches his chair forward and winces as it screeches on the floor. 'But, Dad, it's difficult. I think I'd have to come out. I'd have to tell everyone I'm gay.'

'I'm gay.' Tom can't believe he's just said those words to his dad.

Rod waves his objection away. 'And what's the problem? I want you to do whatever it takes.'

Tom clenches and unclenches his jaw. He tells his dad that he was planning to come out this Saturday – and offers a brief outline of his plan.

'Well, that strikes me as a sound idea,' says Rod. 'You should go ahead.'

'But, Dad, it's the most high-pressured game of my life.'

He doesn't need to remind Rod that, after Toddington won their last game and Arsenal drew, the Toddies are sitting at the top of the Premier League – but only one point clear. Arsenal are playing a low-ranking team in their final game so are predicted to win easily. Whereas Toddington are up against fifth-placed Newcastle United. If they lose, they'll finish second. If they win, the Premier League will be theirs.

Rod shakes his head. 'I don't want to hear it, son. You've given your life to that team. It's time to put yourself first.'

Tom opens his mouth but no words come out.

'Listen to your old dad,' Rod struggles on. 'I want you to come out and fight for whatever you've got with this bloke.'

Tom feels a rush of love for his dad. He wants to hug him but he's worried that Rod's too frail. He settles for resting his hand lightly on top of his.

Rod takes hold of his son's hand and manages to give it a squeeze. 'Before I go,' he says, 'I want to see my lad get all the happiness he deserves.'

14

On the morning of the final match of the season – the match that will decide the winners of the Premier League – Tom drives Isla to her mum's house.

'Today's a big day for Daddy,' he tells her, over his shoulder.

'It's the most important game of your career,' she parrots back at him.

Yeah, he thinks, *but there's something else I need to say* . . .

Tom has puzzled for days over how to tell Isla he's gay. On the one hand, he doesn't want her finding out from media reports – or, even worse, her mother. But on the other hand, he knows she's incapable of keeping a secret, so if he tells her before he's come out publicly, the odds are that she'll immediately go and blab it to Emily. Then his whole plan might fall apart. He might even crack.

'It's also a big day in other ways,' he begins, warily. 'Daddy's got to tell everyone some news. About himself.'

Isla sits up in her booster seat. 'Are you getting married?'

'No, I'm not getting married. But it is about Daddy being happy. And I know you'll like it.'

He pulls up at a red light. Up ahead he can see the floodlights of Toddington's stadium towering over the red-brick terraces around it. Fear catches in his throat.

'So what is it?' Isla asks.

Next to Tom's car, a blue Mazda draws up, driven by a young woman singing along to the radio. 'I can't tell you, pudding. I'd love to, but it's a secret.'

A frown crosses Isla's forehead. 'I don't like secrets. I get excited and want to tell everyone and then I just get into trouble. Like when Sabina told me her mummy had a baby in her tummy and I got told off for telling the class.'

'Exactly. So it's better you don't know; then you can't get into trouble.'

Isla slides her hands under her thighs. 'OK.'

The light turns green and Tom hits the accelerator. 'Thanks for understanding. Now how about I come to Mummy's house and find you after the game?'

Isla puts her head to one side. 'Can we have donuts?'

Tom gives her a smile. 'Yeah, we can have donuts.'

In his Airbnb, Cosmo reads through his interview with Tom. He's sitting at the kitchen table with Isabel and Ruby, who've travelled to Toddington to give him moral support. But he's so nervous he keeps skipping over the words. After failing to take in the same paragraph three times, he decides to read it out loud.

'"I can't wait to take my first truly free kick," Horrocks says as he prepares for the all-important match against Newcastle, "and not just feel proud to be a footballer but also proud to be the first openly gay player in the Premiership. My hope is that I'll inspire all those boys and girls who love football but also know they're different. And one day I'll be able to cheer them on as they too play with pride."'

'That's adorable,' says Isabel, who's wearing a purple neon shell-suit which Cosmo doesn't have the heart to tell her makes her look like a highlighter pen. 'He sounds like a lovely bloke.'

'Yeah, he comes across really well,' agrees Ruby, as she applies a coat of purple lip-gloss. 'Now come and help me choose what to wear.

I want to bag myself a northern lad just like yours.'

Cosmo rolls his eyes affectionately. Before following Ruby through to the bedroom, he sends his article to QueerAndNow's sub-editor to check for typos and errors. He's aware that there's a risk one of his other colleagues might spot it on the system, but this is the most important article of his career. He doesn't want it to contain a single mistake.

He checks his watch; kick-off is in just over three hours.

Which means in roughly four, my story will be going live, he thinks. *And Tom will be making history.*

In Toddington FC's stadium, Tom feels like he's going to throw up. The team are being led through their warm-up by the coaching staff. Although he does every exercise as directed, Tom can't stop thinking about coming out – and worrying that something is going to spoil his plan. He just wants the game to start; then he can forget about it.

He glances up at the stands, which are starting to fill with supporters. *What are they going to say?* he wonders.

'How are you feeling, mate?' asks Uche.

Tom does a lunge and winces. 'My right glute's a bit tight.'

'I'm not talking about your glutes,' Uche says. He lowers his voice. 'I'm talking about your big news.'

Tom does another lunge. 'Mate, I'm trying not to think about it.'

'And now squats!' shouts a coach.

'I can't think of anything *else*,' says Uche, lowering his bum to the ground.

'Uche, you're not helping!' Tom regrets sounding so edgy. 'Sorry, I just don't want us to lose this match because of me. It'll only prove Sergio's point that gay players are a distraction.'

Uche breaks out of the squatting position. 'Mate, that's bullshit! You won't be a distraction *once* you're out of the closet. And you're doing it this way so it *won't* be distracting.'

'What are you girls gossiping about?' interrupts Kyle. 'Do you fancy me? Is that it?'

'Shut it!' Uche barks.

'Oooh, somebody's touchy!' Kyle protests. 'What's up, are you on the rag?'

Uche lowers himself into another squat. 'Give it a rest, Kyle. Isn't it time you switched into beast mode?'

Just as Kyle's responding with his usual roar,

the head coach shouts, 'Fifteen minutes till kick-off! Back to the dressing room, lads!'

Cosmo sits in the stands, watching the game. His heart hammers and adrenaline courses through him.

He can't keep his eyes off Tom. But this time it isn't out of sexual attraction – it's out of concern. *Man,* he thinks, *I hope he can handle this.*

Isabel and Ruby are flirting with two brothers who are sitting in the row behind. They are giggling loudly at everything the men say, prompting hisses of annoyance from other – much more committed – fans. *So much for the moral support, girls!* Cosmo can't help thinking.

Then he tells himself that he's only irritated because he's on edge. He turns back to the pitch.

After fifteen minutes, his phone rings – and Cosmo gives a yelp. Seeing that it's Joshua, he excuses himself and trots up the stairs to a quiet corner of the stadium.

He hits the green button and adopts a cheery tone. 'Hi, Joshua.'

Joshua jabbers, 'Cosmo, the sub just called me. Why didn't you say anything? This is the biggest queer story for years. *Decades!*'

Cosmo frowns. 'That's probably *why* I didn't say anything. It's very sensitive and I feel a duty of care to Tom.'

Joshua rattles on, 'Yeah, but this kind of story needs careful handling. I don't know why you've scheduled it for later – we need to post it now.'

'*Now?*' Cosmo shrieks. 'But I agreed with Tom that we'd post it after the start of the second half.'

'But it's Saturday, Cosmo!' Joshua's starting to sound cross. 'You know our followers switch off after three o'clock. If I'd known, I would have posted it first thing.'

Cosmo gives Joshua a brief run-down of the reasons Tom wants the piece to run later. 'I just can't do that to him.'

Joshua gives a little growl. 'Cosmo, do I have to remind you that your first duty is to your employer? Besides, Tom Horrocks probably won't remember who you are once he's out.'

'Well, actually—'

Cosmo stops himself.

But it's too late.

'Wait a minute,' pipes Josh, 'are you *seeing* this guy?'

Cosmo tugs a hand through his hair. 'Joshua, that's irrelevant. The only thing—'

'I don't believe it!' interrupts Joshua, a note of anger entering his voice. 'Cosmo, I won't have your love life dictating the schedule of my website. I'm bringing the piece forward!'

On the pitch, Tom is playing well. It's a tight match and demanding all his attention. *Which suits me down to the ground*, he thinks.

He stays laser-focused on marking and tracking his man, while keeping an eye on the ball and an awareness of the shifting shape around him. When Newcastle's attackers enter Toddington's half, time after time Tom makes a crunching tackle or intercepts the ball, clearing it into the other team's half. But soon afterwards it always comes back again. Both teams have a robust defence. And despite repeated attempts, neither of them gains any ground. The game is end to end.

When a Newcastle midfielder is injured and the physio rushes on to treat him, Tom suddenly finds his focus wavering. Flashing into his mind comes an image of his dad, watching the game from his hospital bed. He can only imagine how tense he must be feeling.

Oh, Dad, he wants to shout out, *I'm doing my best!*

Then Tom remembers that he doesn't need to play well to earn his dad's love. *Because he loves me anyway*, he realises. *He loves all of me, the real me.*

Something warm blooms in his chest.

Let's hope everyone else feels the same when they hear my news, he thinks.

He wonders how Cosmo's doing and if everything is set up and ready to go. *I'm sure he won't let me down*, he tells himself.

After a few minutes, the injured player is taken off and a substitution made.

As soon as the referee's whistle sounds, Tom's thoughts switch back to football. And he switches back to being a high-performance machine.

'Joshua, you can't do that!' Cosmo argues.

'Can't I?'

Panicked, Cosmo grasps around for a way to stop him. 'If you do, I'll tell Leon we had an affair.'

Joshua snorts. 'Babe, I'll just tell him you're a bunny boiler I shagged a few times. And now I've dumped you, you're out for revenge.'

I *dumped* you, *remember?* Cosmo wants to say. But that would only make things worse.

He has another idea. 'All right, I'll tell him you've been seeing Pete too.'

'Pete?'

'I know all about your latest office liaison. And one affair might be easy to explain, but two's trickier.'

On the other end of the line, Joshua huffs and blows. 'OK, I'll let you post the piece when you want.'

Cosmo gives a little leap. 'Great! Expect it to go live two minutes into the second half.'

'But I'm not happy about it!' Joshua snarls.

Cosmo feels fire building in the pit of his stomach. 'No, but it must be a comfort to know you're doing the right thing – for once.'

Joshua gasps. 'What's that supposed to mean?'

'Look, I've got to go, I've got a football match to watch.' Cosmo can't resist adding, 'But thanks. Thanks, *Josh*.'

The half-time whistle sounds and Tom jogs off the pitch.

With neither team managing to score, there's been no let-up in the tension. *And it's only going to get worse in the second half*, Tom thinks.

But that's nothing compared to the tension that crashes into Tom as he enters the dressing room. And unlike the tension caused by the game, this he doesn't know how to handle. He wishes they didn't have to stop for half time.

The second all the players are assembled, Sergio launches into his pep talk. He tells them Arsenal are winning their game 1–0, so if they end with a goalless draw, Toddington won't win the League. But Tom just cradles his head in his hands and stares at the floor. All he can hear is the roar of his breathing, the blood pounding in his ears.

As soon as Sergio's finished, Tom can't bear the tension any more. He sneaks a glance at his phone.

'We're all set,' reads a text from Cosmo. 'Everything's going to plan.'

Tom's stomach falls away.

'Try not to worry about anything,' Cosmo goes on. 'Just focus on the game. Have a fab second half xx'

Uche leans in and gives Tom's shoulder a bump. 'You've got this, mate.'

Tom's insides give a lurch.

Now can we just get back on the pitch? he wants to cry out.

In the stands, Cosmo feigns interest as Isabel and Ruby introduce him to their new friends.

They're called Clive and Barry and they tell him they aren't really into football but have come to watch because they were born in Toddington and this feels like a historic day.

Oh, you ain't seen nothing yet, he thinks.

Although Clive and Barry seem perfectly nice, Cosmo can't focus on the conversation. He steps back to listen for the referee's whistle. When it finally sounds, an electric pulse runs through him.

Game on!

Cosmo waits for what seems like the longest two minutes of his life, his head spinning with adrenaline.

As soon as his phone shows the time is up, he opens the website that gives him remote access to QueerAndNow. He clicks on his article. And he presses Post.

His stomach does some kind of cartwheel.

This is it, he thinks. *There's no turning back now.*

He looks at Tom powering across the pitch.

The sight of him squeezes at his heart.

15

On the pitch, Tom takes his first truly free kick – and makes history as the first openly gay footballer to play in the Premier League.

As soon as he can get close to him, Uche gives him a pat on the back. 'You did it, mate! Whatever happens now, you did it!'

Tom feels his stomach contract. 'Yep. Now let's win this game.'

Watching from the stands, Cosmo feels tearful with pride. *He's done it*, he thinks. *He's just taken one of the last strongholds of homophobia and smashed through it.*

Within minutes, Cosmo can tell from his social media that the story has exploded.

'What a hero!' tweets a popular sports reporter.

'Such an inspiration!' an Olympian comments on Instagram.

Cosmo also notices that his accounts are amassing new followers – amongst them the editor of the *Guardian*. He hopes she's impressed.

In the stands around him, people are snatching a look at their phones.

'Here, have you seen this?' Clive says to Barry.

Barry reads the headline. 'Good on him!'

'As long as he keeps playing well,' interrupts a man next to them, 'I couldn't care less if Tom Horrocks does the can-can naked down Toddington High Street.'

Cosmo suppresses a chuckle. *I don't think there's much chance of that*, he thinks.

On the pitch, Tom doesn't even think about how people are responding to his news.

As the minutes tick away, the tension continues to rise. Soon, the players are snapping at each other – some of them physically lashing out. Disaster strikes when Kyle fouls a Newcastle player and is given a red card. He's sent off; Toddington are one man down.

Tom's heart dives to his stomach. *Shit,* he thinks, *how are we supposed to win now?*

To his surprise, Sergio beckons him over, along with Uche, as team captain.

'Lads,' he bellows, 'Arsenal are 2–0 up. We need to do something drastic. We need a goal.'

Tom and Uche nod, grimly.

Sergio puts his hands on his hips. 'Tom, I want you to move up front.'

Tom's mouth falls open. 'What?'

'Look, I know it's a gamble but we need your strength and height in the other half. Can you handle it?'

Tom drags in a long breath.

Uche lays a hand on his shoulder. 'Yeah, he can handle it.'

'Tom?'

Tom exhales. 'Yep, I'll do it.'

'Good lad!'

He turns and trots back onto the pitch.

What happens next seems almost hyperreal, as if Tom is seeing it in high-definition or through a supersharp filter.

He powers down the pitch, switching from defence mode into attack. As his body thrums with the cheers of the crowd, he and Uche push forward, passing the ball to each other. They steer it towards Newcastle's box several times, but each time Tom passes the ball to Uche he fails to score.

They enter injury time.

Come on, Tom, he tells himself. *It's now or never.*

With seconds to go, Tom once again steers the ball into the penalty area and passes it to Uche. Uche is tackled by two defenders and – to avoid losing possession – boots the ball back in Tom's direction. But his pass is long and high. Surrounded by Newcastle defenders, Tom knows he can only respond in one way.

He wrestles clear of the opposition, leaps high into the air and connects perfectly with the ball, heading it down and into the back of the net.

'*Goal!*'

The crowd roar so loudly that for a second Tom thinks a bomb may have gone off.

His teammates crowd around him, hugging and patting him, then lift him high in the air.

'Fuck me!' splutters Uche. 'That was unreal!'

Just as Tom's being lowered to the ground, the final whistle blows – although it can barely be heard under the roar of the home crowd.

Toddington FC have won the match. They've won the Premier League.

Cosmo never thought he could get so caught up in a game of football, but Tom's goal made him cheer out loud *and* brought him to tears. He thinks it was possibly the most thrilling, beautiful thing he's ever seen.

And man, he thinks, *what a way to prove a point!*

All around him, the supporters are chanting,

'Horrocks Rocks! Horrocks Rocks! Horrocks Rocks!'

He can't help imagining how Tom's coming out – coupled with his heroism on the pitch – is being greeted outside the stadium, by queer kids up and down the country. *What he's done today is going to change so much*, he thinks.

'Well done, mate!' says Isabel. 'You did it!'

Cosmo shrugs. 'Oh, it wasn't me, it was all Tom.' Just saying his name, he feels a swell of pride.

'So what happens now?' interjects Ruby.

Cosmo explains that he's meeting Tom outside the home dressing room – but Jackie only gave him one pass. 'I'm sorry but I've got to go on my own.'

'Don't worry, babes,' Ruby chirps, 'Clive and Barry have invited us out for drinks.'

Isabel gives him a wink. 'We figured you'd be otherwise engaged.'

Once he's said his goodbyes, Cosmo weaves his way through the sea of supporters, down through the stands and into what he calls the backstage area.

He settles on the edge of a huddle of people waiting outside the dressing room. He doesn't want to push himself to the front. *It's not as if I'm Tom's boyfriend or anything*, he tells himself.

Hope catches in his chest.

Although now he's out of the closet, Cosmo thinks, *who knows what'll happen?*

In the dressing room, the Toddies are celebrating their win – surrounded by the staff who've helped them to success. Champagne shoots out of bottles, arms are stretched around shoulders, and there's rowdy singing around the theme of champions.

One by one, Tom's teammates come over to congratulate him on his goal – and also his personal news.

'Respect for being so honest,' says one.

'What you did was bare brave,' adds another.

As he towels his hair dry, Kyle approaches him. 'Sorry I was a dick earlier. And sorry if I've been a dick in the past. You're a top bloke, Tom. I really admire what you've done.'

Tom is surprised but touched. 'Thanks, Kyle. I appreciate that.'

In Sergio's victory speech – delivered between swigs of champagne and bouts of cheering – he also refers to Tom's news. 'A special well done to Tom not just for scoring the winning goal but also for coming out of the closet.'

There's more cheering.

Sergio fixes Tom with his eyes. 'I wish you'd tipped me off beforehand, although I was that stressed I'm not sure my heart would have taken it. Anyway, thanks for doing it in a way that didn't distract from the football.'

'You know what, I think it actually *boosted* his playing!' jokes Kyle.

'I guess that's what happens when you're true to yourself,' says Uche.

'Well, if anyone else wants to be true to themselves,' Sergio quips, 'you have my full approval!'

Sergio presents Tom with the ball from the match to keep as a souvenir – an honour usually reserved for players who've scored a hat trick.

Tom feels overwhelmed. This is everything he ever wanted from football, but it's also everything he didn't even know he wanted *outside* the game. As he holds up the ball, tears prickle the backs of his eyes.

'Horrocks Rocks!' chant his teammates. 'Horrocks Rocks! Horrocks Rocks!'

After a while, Tom manages to deflect the attention back onto the team's win.

I need to see Cosmo, he thinks.

Just as he's wondering how he can slip outside, his phone rings. It's his agent.

Tom answers and hears that the board of

Toddington FC are thrilled with his personal news as they want to publicly show off their commitment to inclusion. Apparently, the FA has already asked if Tom will front a major campaign celebrating diversity in football. And on top of that, he's being swamped with offers from sponsors.

Tom can't help feeling a flicker of fear. 'That sounds like a lot,' he says. 'Do I have to do it all?'

'Tom, you can do as little or as much of it as you want,' his agent reassures him. 'And you don't need to decide now. Why don't you take some time to think about it?'

Tom nods. 'Yeah, OK.'

'You never know, you might feel differently about putting yourself out there now you've nothing to hide.'

When Tom finally makes it outside, Emily and Isla are waiting at the front of the crowd. As he's greeted by a chorus of cheers, Isla comes running towards him. He lifts her high in the air, savouring the sound of her giggles.

'Hiya, pudding! I didn't know you guys were coming!'

'Daddy, you're gay like Albert and George!' Isla bursts out. 'That means you're a hero too!'

'Oh, I don't know about that,' Tom says, swinging her down and balancing her on his hip.

'You *are* a hero,' Emily chips in. 'As soon as we heard the news we had to come down.'

Tom lowers Isla to the floor. 'I was going to come over and see you tonight.'

'I know, but I didn't want to wait that long.' Emily tucks a strand of hair behind her ear. 'Look, I'm sorry I've been so hard on you.'

'Don't be daft, Em. You weren't to know. And let's be honest, I should have got my head together sooner.'

Emily waves away his comment. 'You had a lot going on, Tom. I can see that now. We'll obviously talk properly soon, but I just want to say I hope we can build a new relationship – as friends.'

Just as Tom is replying that he'd like that very much, Isla interrupts. 'Daddy, when are you going to get a boyfriend?'

Tom chortles. 'One step at a time!' Then he leans down to whisper in her ear, 'But between us, I'm working on it.'

As he straightens himself up, over Emily's shoulder he spots Cosmo. He feels slightly woozy.

Come on, Tom, he tells himself. *Get it together.*

'There's someone else who wants to speak to you,' Emily says, tapping on her phone.

She hands it to Tom and he sees his dad, propped up in his hospital bed. 'Dad! How are you feeling?'

A grin illuminates Rod's face. 'A lot better after that goal, son. And your beltin' news! Never mind t'cancer, I feel like I could lift a jumbo jet!'

Tom laughs. 'Steady on, Dad. I need you out of that hospital in one piece!'

Rod nods, firmly. 'Seriously, though, I couldn't be prouder.'

Once again, Tom has to fight back the tears. 'Thanks, Dad.'

'Now remember what I told you t'other day,' Rod adds. 'And go and get your man!'

As Tom walks towards him, Cosmo's heart gives a wobble. It feels as if they're meeting for the first time.

Despite being desperate to see him, suddenly Cosmo doesn't know what to say.

'Hi!' he blurts out.

He becomes aware of people glancing over – and doesn't want to embarrass Tom. *I don't want to push him too far*, he thinks.

'Well done,' he manages, rocking backwards and forwards on the balls of his feet. 'You had an incredible game.'

Tom kneads his knuckles; he must be feeling just as awkward as Cosmo. 'Thanks. I couldn't have done it without you.'

'Oh, I can't take any credit for that header,' Cosmo jokes, weakly.

'No, but you can for the way I was feeling.' Tom looks down and bumps his toes against the floor. 'Anyway, I just wanted to say—'

'There you are!'

They're interrupted by Jackie, who delivers the news that Tom has won Man of the Match.

In an instant, his nerves are wiped out by a smile. 'Wow, can today get any better?'

Jackie takes hold of his elbow. 'Come on, I need to get you to the presentation.'

'Oh.' Tom's forehead crinkles. 'Can I just quickly speak to Cosmo? There's something I've got to say.'

Cosmo's heart takes flight. *Oh yeah*, he wonders, *what's that?*

Jackie flashes them a wry smile. 'You know, I could tell something was going on between you two! But sorry, flower, they need you now. We're live in a few minutes.'

114

'Shit, right.' Tom turns to Cosmo. 'I won't be long.'

'That's all right,' says Cosmo. 'Do whatever you need.'

Jackie steers Tom off towards the tunnel. 'Don't stand there gawping!' she shouts back at Cosmo. 'Come with us!'

As the cameras roll, the sports correspondent steps back to let Uche – as captain of the winning team – present Tom with the award for Man of the Match.

'Can I just say what an honour it is to play alongside a man of such integrity,' he declares. 'A man who put himself on the line to right a major wrong, a man who took a big risk to send a message of hope out to the world.'

Tom feels as if he's glowing with pride. He sees Cosmo standing behind the crew, watching.

An idea jumps into his head.

But can I . . .? he thinks.

'Thanks, mate,' Tom says. 'But it's only fair that I also thank the man who made me want to right that wrong. And that's the journalist who helped tell my story, Cosmo Roberts.'

Tom beckons Cosmo over and the crew and club media team turn to look at him.

Man, he thinks, *what's going on?*

'Although Cosmo isn't just a journalist,' Tom says to the camera. 'He's also very special to me.'

He holds out his hand. Cosmo steps in front of the camera and takes it.

'Cosmo, I know we said we'd keep my story separate to what's happening between me and you . . .' Tom continues, trying not to let his voice crack.

Cosmo blinks. 'Yeah?' *Is he seriously going to do this?* he asks himself.

Tom pauses and reminds himself that his words are broadcasting live to millions of people. And not just that, but clips of this will make news bulletins around the world – and may be replayed for the rest of his life.

I'm keeping going, he decides.

'Now I've kicked down the door of my closet,' he says, 'I'm free to explore my feelings. And I'd like to explore my feelings for you. Will you be my boyfriend?'

Cosmo's eyes twinkle. 'Yes. Of course I will!'

And – as the world watches – the two men kiss.

About Quick Reads

"Reading is such an important building block for success"
~ Jojo Moyes

Quick Reads are short books written
by best-selling authors.

Did you enjoy this Quick Read?

Tell us what you thought by filling in
our short survey. Scan the **QR code**
to go directly to the survey or
visit **bit.ly/QR2024**

Thanks to Penguin Random House and Hachette and to all
our publishing partners for their ongoing support.

A special thank you to Jojo Moyes for her generous donation in
2020–2022 which helped to build the future of Quick Reads.

Quick Reads is delivered by The Reading Agency, a UK charity
with a mission to get people fired up about reading, because
everything changes when you read.

www.readingagency.org.uk @readingagency #QuickReads

The Reading Agency Ltd. Registered number: 3904882 (England & Wales)
Registered charity number: 1085443 (England & Wales)
Registered Office: 24 Bedford Row, London, WC1R 4EH
The Reading Agency is supported using public funding by
Arts Council England.

THE READING AGENCY | **Quick Reads**

Find your next Quick Read...

For 2024 we have selected six popular
Quick Reads for you to enjoy!

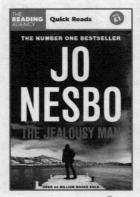

Quick Reads are available to buy in paperback or ebook and to borrow from your local library. For a complete list of titles and more information on the authors and their books visit **www.readingagency.org.uk/quickreads**

Continue your reading journey with The Reading Agency:

Reading Ahead

Challenge yourself to complete six reads by taking part in **Reading Ahead** at your local library, college or workplace: **readingahead.org.uk**

Reading
Groups
for Everyone

Join **Reading Groups for Everyone** to find a reading group and discover new books: **readinggroups.org.uk**

World Book Night

Celebrate reading on **World Book Night** every year on 23 April: **worldbooknight.org**

Summer Reading Challenge

Read with your family as part of the **Summer Reading Challenge: summerreadingchallenge.org.uk**

For more information on our work and the power of reading please visit our website: **readingagency.org.uk**

More from Quick Reads

If you enjoyed the 2024 Quick Reads please explore our 6 titles from 2023.

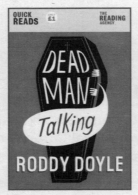

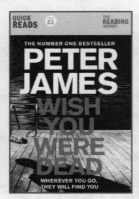

For a complete list of titles and more information on the authors and their books visit:
www.readingagency.org.uk/quickreads

Discover more from Matt Cain . . .

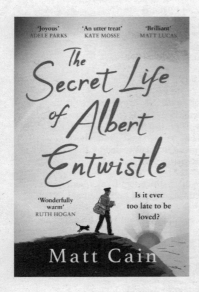

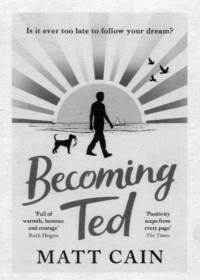

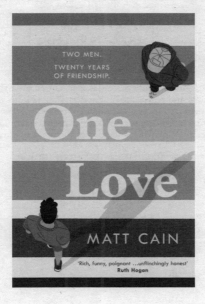

This Quick Reads edition first published in paperback in Great Britain in 2024
by HEADLINE REVIEW
An imprint of HEADLINE PUBLISHING GROUP

1

Cataloguing in Publication Data is available from the British Library

Paperback ISBN 978 1 0354 0973 0

Typeset in Stone Serif by CC Book Production

Printed and bound in Great Britain by Clays Ltd, Elcograf S.p.A.

HEADLINE PUBLISHING GROUP
An Hachette UK Company
Carmelite House
50 Victoria Embankment
London EC4Y 0DZ

www.headline.co.uk
www.hachette.co.uk